The Case of the Terminated Tattler

When Albert finally reached the room he found the reveller slumped forward, across the blotter, evidently in a drunken stupor. The room reeked of alcohol and the bottle of port had fallen over. A red stain had formed on the carpet and liquid still dripped on it steadily. Albert, who had seen it all before many times, sighed and strode toward the desk. Only when his shout of "Come along now, Mr. Derby, taxi's here" had failed three times did he attempt to shake the body into activity. When he did he instantly recoiled.

St. John Derby was not drunk. He was, of course, extremely dead.

DEADLINE

Tim Heald

BALLANTINE BOOKS • NEW YORK

FOR EMMA

Prologue

The annual extraordinary dinner of the Worshipful Company of Master Harbingers had been, as usual, sumptuous. In a changing and hostile world the Harbingers, whose principal claim to fame was their preposterous prosperity, had the good sense to dispense copious food and drink to selected members of the outside world once a year. It stopped the world from judging too harshly their unlovely avarice. By stuffing the editor of *The Times* with quail and by pouring Château Lafite down the throat of the Archbishop, the Harbingers managed to avoid censure for a policy unique among the great livery companies of the City of London. They dispensed no charity. They lived for themselves alone, except for the annual thrash on the Thursday after Epiphany.

Shortly after eleven o'clock that evening St John Derby, the editor of the Samuel Pepys column of the *Daily Globe*, was stumbling uncertainly down Ludgate Hill. He had been making very free with the hospitality of the Harbingers, a hospitality he earned carefully by writing frequent flattering stories about the company in his daily diary. His cloak flapped behind him in the crisp January air and his heavy stick beat an irregular pattern on the pavement, his sixty-year-old face was more than usually purple and there was armagnac on his shirtfront. A taxi was what he wanted but no taxi came. Most had been grabbed on behalf of more distinguished guests of the Harbingers or by younger, swifter, less inebriated gossip columnists. He sighed and staggered on.

At Ludgate Circus he paused for a moment. Had he turned left he could have walked to Blackfriars and taken the District line underground to South Kensington, a mere three minutes' walk from his flat. Instead he lurched over the road and continued straight on up Fleet Street. After a hundred yards he turned left into an impressive grey slab which could have been designed by Mussolini, nodded at the uniformed doorman and took the lift to the fifth floor. Once there he turned right along a panelled passage and stopped outside a heavy door on which his own and Samuel Pepys' names appeared in bold black.

He fumbled for a few moments with his keys, let himself in and sat down heavily at his desk. After a little more fumbling he produced another key and unlocked the bottom right drawer from which he took a bottle of Sandeman's port. With an unsteady hand he poured a generous measure into a tumbler on the desk, then picked up the internal phone and dialled down to the front hall.

'Any chance of a taxi to Kensington, Albert?' he asked.

They were the last words anyone heard him speak. More than an hour later Albert, who had had his attention distracted and who had in any case found taxis hard to come by, tried to reach Derby on the telephone. Failing, he argued, not unreasonably, that the celebrated diarist must have fallen asleep at his desk, and decided to call personally to wake him.

When he finally reached the room he found the reveller slumped forward across the blotter, evidently in a drunken stupor. The room reeked of alcohol and the bottle of port had fallen over. A red stain had formed on the carpet and liquid still dripped on to it steadily. Albert, who had seen it all before many times, sighed and strode towards the desk. Only when his shout of 'Come along now, Mr Derby, taxi's here' had failed three times did he attempt to shake the body into activity. When he did he instantly recoiled.

St John Derby was not just drunk. He was, of course, extremely dead.

1

The death of their leader did not come as an over-whelming shock to the small team who daily produced the Samuel Pepys column. It came first to Eric Gringe at his home in Bromley. 'Oh Lord,' he said to his wife Thelma when the phone rang. 'I knew it. It'll be some-thing to do with that piece on the Anglo-Rhodesian Friendship society. I told St John to leave it out.' A moment later he said simply, 'Oh dear. How shocking. I'll come right in. Oh all right then . . . nine sharp . . . in your office.'

After he'd rung off Mr Gringe sat up in bed and put on the bedside lamp. 'I'm going to make a cup of tea,' he said, 'St John Derby's dead.'

His wife stirred at his side. 'Mmmm?'

'Dead. St John.' Mr Gringe put a hand inside the jacket of his pyjamas and scratched abstractedly. 'It would be the drink of course,' he said. 'I'm amazed it didn't happen sooner but the way he abused himself it's hardly surprising.'

Mrs Gringe sat up beside her husband.

'What a dreadful thing,' she said. 'Does that mean you'll take over?'

Mr Gringe made a face. 'Really, Thelma, I think you ought to have a little more respect. He only died an hour or so ago.'

'He's been dead from the neck up for the last fifteen years at least, as you well know. You've said as much time and again. If it hadn't been for all the work you put in on that column he'd have been sacked years ago.'

Mr Gringe who was a conscientious forty-five knew it perfectly well.

'I'll be in charge until they find someone else of course,' he said.

3

His wife grimaced. 'Eric Gringe,' she said, 'you let them ride over you, you do really. There's no reason on earth why they should find someone else. You've a right to that job. You've earned it.'

Mr Gringe looked at his watch. It was six. 'I'll go and get that tea,' he said, 'then I'll tell the others. I've got to be in the Managing Editor's office at nine.'

The first call was to Molly Mortimer. All the time he was making the tea, getting the Garibaldi biscuits out of the tin, and emptying the dog, he was wondering in what order he ought to tell his colleagues. It would have been simpler and more effective to tell them all at once as soon as he'd seen Clapham, the Managing Editor, but that would be too late. By then the rumours would be spreading up Fleet Street, distorting in and out of other newspaper offices, garbling at early morning press receptions ready for the full scandalous blast of half-truth which would come as soon as the pubs opened. No, he would have to telephone.

Upstairs again he dropped crumbs on the sheets and decided to begin with Molly Mortimer. Nobody could complain if he began with the column's woman. He looked the number up in the back of his diary where it was pencilled in his neat cramped clerk's handwriting. She had a flat just behind Sloane Square. He and Thelma had been there once for cocktails. It had been full of mirrors, and Thelma, who had left her coat in the bedroom, had pronounced it scandalous.

He dialled and waited while the phone at the other end rang for an age. Just as he was about to give up it stopped and a man's voice said, 'For Christ's sake. Have you *any* idea what the time is?' It sounded to Gringe suspiciously like young Willy Wimbledon but the idea was ridiculous.

'This is very important,' said Gringe, 'is Miss Mortimer there?'

'Hang on. Who is it?'

'Eric Gringe.'

There was a pause and then Molly's throaty voice saying 'Darling, whatever is it? It is dreadfully early.'

'I'm sorry, Molly,' he said, 'I just thought you ought to know that St John's been found dead.'

A short silence, then. 'Oh darling. How frightful. Can I help? I mean what would you like me to do?'

This slightly nonplussed him. 'Nothing much we can do,' he said, 'but I'm asking you all to come in to the office at half past nine for a conference. Is that all right?'

'Is that all?' She sounded disappointed.

'Yes. Can you manage it?'

'I did have breakfast arranged at the Connaught but I shall just have to cancel. What was it? Stroke?'

'I don't know. I should think so.'

'So should I. See you at nine-thirty.'

Next, partly so as to dismiss the absurd suspicion, still lurking irrelevantly at the back of his mind, he called Viscount Wimbledon's number. There was no reply. The suspicion advanced.

It occurred to him that the Honourable Bertie Harris might already have heard of the tragedy. As the son and heir of the *Globe*'s proprietor, the first Baron Wharfedale, he was often privy to information which was not advanced to relatively junior members of the staff such as Eric Gringe. This did not improve his relations with such people in general nor with Mr Gringe in particular.

'Ah . . .' he said when he heard his colleague say a brusque 'Harris', in answer to the ringing tone. 'Ah . . . have you heard the sad news?'

'Sad news, what sad news? I'm still in bed so of course I haven't heard any news, sad or otherwise. It's not my habit to hear news until I wake which thanks to you I now have. So tell me, what sad news?'

'St John Derby has passed away.' Mr Gringe had no idea why he used the silly euphemism. Bertie Harris always forced him into self parody.

'Some would say that that is neither sad nor news,' said Lord Wharfedale's heir. 'I can't say I find it hard to believe though I could perhaps, if pressed, muster the merest twinge of regret.'

'I'm asking everyone to come into the office at nine-thirty for a chat,' said Gringe, lamely. 'Can you manage it?'

'I'll be there. Good morning.'

Mrs. Gringe looked at him with some contempt. 'You should stand up to them, Eric. You really should,' she said.

He said nothing but dialled the number for Milborn Port, the last member of the Pepys team who inhabited a *bijou* residence overlooking Stoke Poges golf club.

'Good God,' said Milborn when the news had finally permeated to his brain, 'so the grape got him in the end. Poor old sod. There but for the grace of God . . .'

'Can you be in at nine-thirty?'

'It'll be the first time for twenty years, but I'll make it. I think we owe it to the old boy, out of respect.'

Eric Gringe drank the last of his milky tea. It was too bad about Willy Wimbledon. He wondered if he ought to tell Anthea Morrison, the secretary, but decided to postpone it till later. It would not be proper for her to be at the meeting so there was no particular hurry. As for Horace Peckwater, the sub-editor, he could wait too. He certainly wasn't having any tuppeny-ha'penny sub-editor at a writers' meeting.

It was after seven now and outside the Gringe semi, Bromley was beginning to stir. Mr Gringe went to the wardrobe and selected an appropriate tie, the only one he had which meant anything, his RAC tie, then he took of his striped pyjama top, slipped on a string vest and went to shave. With a tremor of guilt he realized that he was feeling strangely excited, even exhilarated, at the prospect of the day ahead.

Later that morning he emerged from the Managing Editor's office, white faced and trembling. It had been a distressing interview. Short and to the point but definitely distressing. As it was only nine-fifteen he went across the road and bought a cup of coffee in a plastic cup to steady his nerves. Back in the Pepys office he noticed that St John's desk had been cleared and a hole cut in the carpet immediately next to his chair. There was also a lot of grey powder about the place which Clapham had said, with a touch of melodrama, was to do with finger printing. For a moment Mr Gringe wondered whether it would be proper for him to sit at St John's desk as he normally did when he was deputizing for his chief but decided against it, as Milborn Port would have put it, 'Out of respect for the old boy'.

He felt rather sick.

His colleagues arrived singly. Harris first, smirking as usual, then Molly Mortimer, then Port and finally, to his surprise, a breathless Willy Wimbledon.

'Who told you we were convening?' he asked him tetchily, but before the Viscount could reply, Miss Mortimer chipped in. '*I* did, Eric. I had a feeling you might forget the new boy so I rang him to make sure and I was absolutely right. Very naughty of you.'

'I tried to ring you,' he said crossly, 'but there was no reply. None at all.'

'You must have mis-dialled,' said Wimbledon, grinning boyishly. 'It happens a lot.'

'I did *not* mis-dial,' said Gringe, his voice rising a dangerous octave. 'I quite definitely did not mis-dial.' He stopped and took a breath. 'I'm sorry,' he said, 'I'm afraid I've been more affected by what's happened than perhaps I realized. You're probably right. I probably mis-dialled.'

'Anyway,' said Bertie Harris, 'let's get on with it. I rather gather there's more to this business than meets the eye. Are you going to do some explaining, old boy?'

Mr Gringe fingered his RAC tie and tried to glower menacingly. The effect was simply one of extreme petulance.

'You seem to know a lot, Harris,' he said. 'Perhaps you'd like to tell us yourself?'

Harris shrugged. 'You're in charge and I understand that Martin Clapham's put you in the picture . . . well,' he coughed deprecatingly, 'well into some of the picture at least, so I suggest you tell us whatever it is that you feel you ought to tell us.'

'For God's sake get on with it,' said Milborn Port.

Eric Gringe flushed. 'Originally,' he said, 'I just wanted to meet like this so that we could discuss arrangements for producing the column over the next few days, and also so that we could decide what sort of arrangements we ought to make for the deceased. You know he didn't have any family and in a way I think perhaps he looked on us as his family and therefore it seemed only proper that perhaps we ought to make some special effort, and assume some special responsibility for making sure that everything is done properly. He'd have wanted everything done properly. It would have been important to him so I think that it should be important to us too. But . . . but, I'm afraid Mr Clapham has told me something which while it doesn't make any real difference to any of that, is still, er, more important. Well, immediately important.' He paused and looked at his colleagues. 'You see,' he said, 'poor old St John didn't have a stroke at all. He didn't die from natural causes of any sort. He was stabbed. With a paper knife.'

2

Simon Bognor was also summoned to an unexpected meeting that morning. He was lying half asleep in the bed he shared with his longstanding girl friend Monica, reading *The Times* while she scrambled eggs in the distance. As usual he began at the end, with the obituaries, and was on the point of entertaining her with a recitation of the salient points in the career of a West Indian diplomat who had been assassinated the previous day while shopping in Regent Street when the phone rang.

'Parkinson,' he moaned, 'two to one on Parkinson.

Nobody but Parkinson would ring like that. So shrill and aggressive.'

'For heaven's sake answer it,' shouted Monica, emerging briefly from the kitchenette, hands full of saucepan and wooden spoon. Obediently he went lethargically to the instrument.

'Bognor,' said Parkinson, 'you are indolent and slothful and by this time of the morning you should be sufficiently wide awake to answer the telephone before it has rung three times.'

'I was in the middle of my press-ups,' said Bognor looking down at his thickening waist and thinking that the idea was not a bad one.

'I am in the office at this moment, Bognor, and I want you round here in half an hour at the latest. Can you do shorthand?'

'No.'

'Type?'

'One hand and two fingers.'

'It'll have to do. You're going to spend some time on a newspaper, though, so help me God, it's no wish of mine that you should. I will see you here in twenty-eight minutes.' The line clicked and Parkinson's voice vanished.

'Funny,' said Bognor. He sauntered into the kitchen and kissed Monica idly on the cheek. 'Parkinson wants me to be a journalist. At least I think he does.'

'What's journalism got to do with the Board of Trade?'

'I should know in about twenty-five minutes.'

Because of the unwonted urgency Bognor splurged on a taxi. Normally he was more cautious. The Board of Trade did not pay its investigators handsomely, and although Bognor had been with the organization for some years he had not obtained preferment. It was painfully obvious to all concerned that Bognor's talents, whatever they might be, were wasted in the Special Operations department of the Ministry. The qualities demanded of men in the Department were patience and courage, ruthlessness and cunning. Simon

Bognor was impatient and cowardly, squeamish and utterly straightforward. He was poor at poker, increasingly fat and florid. Years before, his honest degree and his guileless manner had plainly qualified him for the conventional Civil Service career which all about him had predicted. Then at that fateful interview with the University Appointments Officer he had made that totally whimsical error. It was still etched on his mind. He could see the stiff donnish figure leaning across the table at him and saying 'There is *another* branch of the Civil Service, a rather special Branch.' He dreamt about it sometimes but even in his dreams his own response was the same: an eager nod, an indication of genuine enthusiasm and real intent. Then the ensuing nightmare of week-end house-parties and mysterious men in pubs in macs. Later decoding, and reading ciphers and debriefing people and suddenly that dreadful experience of being sent out on his own to investigate the mystery of the smuggled secrets from Beaubridge Friary, and then the even worse affair of the murdered peers and the Umdaka of Mangolo. He shuddered at the memory and paid off the taxi.

Trotting downstairs he wondered what on earth Parkinson had been on about. After the last case, from which despite some undeniable *faux pas* he and the department had emerged, Bognor reckoned, with no little credit, Parkinson had vowed to keep him chained to his desk for ever and ever, never to be allowed out on even the most menial errand. Secretly Bognor was pleased. He was not ambitious.

Outside Parkinson's office he stopped for a moment, pulled at his tie, patted his jowls, smoothed the thinning hair which stuck up rebelliously at the back, and then knocked.

'Come.'

Bognor waited and counted to ten. He delayed partly because he was afraid and partly to annoy. As he finally entered Parkinson was in the middle of saying 'Come' for the second time.

'Why,' he snapped, 'are you incapable of coming

when I say "come", I shall never understand. However there are many other things I fear I shall never understand and most of them concern you, Bognor. Sit down.'

Bognor sat and stared thoughtfully and apprehensively at his chief's steely eyes and impatient mouth.

'What do you have in mind for me . . . sir?'

Parkinson twitched. 'I personally have nothing much in mind for you. Others evidently do. You've heard of Lord Wharfedale?'

'Of course.'

'You know that he owns the *Globe* Group?'

'Yes.'

'And that the *Globe* sponsors the Expo-Brit scheme in which you became so hopelessly embroiled while investigating—if that is the correct word—the agricultural secrets which were being smuggled to Eastern Europe?'

'Yes.' Bognor was very perplexed indeed.

'It appears, and I don't have to tell you that I find this most surprising, it appears that his Lordship was exceedingly impressed with the way in which you handled the case.'

Bognor *was* surprised.

'So impressed,' continued Parkinson, 'that when a member of his own staff is found murdered at Wharfedale House he is not satisfied with the perfectly adequate measures being taken by the excellent Criminal Investigation Department of the City Police. No, not a bit of it. So he immediately telephones the Minister, who is naturally a very old friend, or to be more accurate, is naturally a politician to whom a kind word from the *Daily Globe* means a great deal and he says to him—and here my comprehension is strained to its very limits—and says to him, "I want Simon Bognor of the Board of Trade assigned to this case".'

Bognor couldn't help smiling. It had been his first case.

'What exactly does he want me to do?'

'He wants you to join the Samuel Pepys column of

the *Daily Globe*. After the murder they're one short and I gather they're rather given to employing people of limited experience.' He managed to imply 'and of little ability' without actually saying it.

'I'm sorry, you haven't told me yet who's been killed.'

Parkinson smiled bleakly. 'A man called St John Derby. He ran the Pepys column. Had done for years.'

'Wasn't he what's known as a character?'

'I think,' Parkinson seemed relaxed for the first time that morning, 'that Lord Wharfedale described him as "a journalist of the old school". He was about sixty. Married once, years ago, unsatisfactorily to Lotte Pelman, the woman who's on all those TV quizzes. Lived on his own in South Kensington. Drank excessively, played a certain amount of bridge, moderately gregarious, belonged to the Savage Club and Surrey County Cricket Club. Inordinately fond of cricket I believe. And reputed to know most of the work of G.K. Chesterton by heart.'

'I'm sure I've come across him somewhere,' said Bognor. 'Didn't he wear peculiar clothes?'

'He affected a cloak and a wide brimmed black hat. And he used to carry a stick.'

'I know,' said Bognor, with an air of triumph, 'I've seen him in the back of El Vino's drinking champagne. Fat chap.'

'Inclined to obesity.'

'How was he killed?'

'Stabbed with a paper knife late last night or early this morning. They found it behind a radiator. No prints, just some glovemarks.'

'Any thoughts?'

'None whatever.'

'Is it of any interest to the Department? I mean he wasn't in espionage or anything? No security leaks?'

'It's only of interest because you have been assigned to the matter. You were not assigned because of any interest on my part. As so often where you are concerned, Bognor, my sole concern is that the affair should be concluded without embarrassment. Please.'

'When do I start?'

'Lord Wharfedale would like to see you first. At ten. He apparently wishes you to preserve your incognito. You are not to be recognized as an investigator of any sort, you are to convince everyone that you are a bona fide journalist.'

'How?'

'That's your problem.'

'Do they know the old man was murdered?' Bognor felt out of his depth already.

'At first the Wharfedale management thought they might be able to hush it up but eventually they decided against. The doorman found him and there was rather a lot of blood. The old pals act will operate as far as the press is concerned. "Journalist found dead" I assume, with a strong suggestion of suicide. The inquest will be adjourned as long as necessary—that's arranged. But most of the staff of the *Globe* will know. The staff of the column—your new colleagues'—he smiled again, 'have been told officially. Because all journalists and particularly, I believe, those who work on gossip columns are incapable of keeping secrets I should imagine that all Fleet Street will know it was murder by now.'

'Ah.'

Interview over, Bognor went briefly to his desk to collect his thoughts and the morning mail. This did not sound an entertaining assignment. His experience of journalism was entirely vicarious, at least since Oxford when he had written occasional drama notes for *Isis*. Some of his university contemporaries had taken it up but it had proved bad for their marriages and worse for their livers. Those that he still saw also seemed to have become quite unnecessarily cynical and world weary.

The *Globe* was not regular reading for Bognor and he hadn't so much as glanced at the Samuel Pepys column since it had carried an item about the occasion on which he and some friends had planted turf and daffodils in Trinity Senior Common Room. That was more than ten years ago. Nevertheless the Department library had all the morning papers so before setting off for Lord Wharfedale's he went there to refresh his memory.

The *Globe* was a broadsheet, the same size as *The Times* or the *Daily Telegraph* which it resembled in no other way. Its politics under the aegis of the ageing Wharfedale were well to the right of either but were inspired by a Calvinist zeal which the proprietor was thought to have acquired in his native South Africa where he was brought up in the religion of the Dutch Reform Church. The *Globe* was reactionary but it made its appeal to 'the man in the street'. Leader writers were instructed to refer frequently to the benefits of thrift and industry and to spice their texts with frequent references to 'ordinary folk'. The rest of the paper was given over to a spirited examination of contemporary society which spared a few of the more lurid details while, of course, always deploring them. The style was floridly old fashioned and nowhere more so than on the Samuel Pepys column which combined the worst of its principal rivals, the William Hickey column of the *Daily Express* and the Peterborough column of the *Telegraph*.

That morning's, the last to appear under the editorship of St John Derby, had approximately ten items in all: a joke about the price of steak which Bognor was sure he had seen elsewhere, a cartoon which showed two men in hats and bore the caption 'I suppose before long with student grants increasing at 12 per cent they really will be able to have their cake and eat it', which he found totally incomprehensible. There was a story about the 105th birthday of the Colonel-in-Chief of the Royal Wiltshire Yeomanry; an account of the Harbingers' dinner; a suggestion that there was a split in the Anglo-Rhodesian Friendship Society; a very ambiguous innuendo hinting that the teenage daughter of a minor canon of Salisbury cathedral might be the result of an adulterous liaison between her mother and a notorious cabinet minister; a speculative piece about the secretaryship of Pring's and a very clear suggestion that Lady Aubergine Bristol had been incapably drunk at the annual Instamex Literary luncheon. Bognor sighed. He very much doubted whether he would be able to master the breathless 'Strange goings-on at the annual Instamex luncheon yesterday!' any more than 'Sir Cedric Ponsonby, K.B.E., tells me he will be 105 on Thursday and assures me he is as fit as the proverbial fiddle, a fact he attributes to his unusual diet of bananas and turbot with a glass of madeira every morning at eleven'. He sighed again. It was time to be moving in the direction of Lord Wharfedale.

Once more he took a taxi. He had the impression that journalists travelled everywhere by taxi and were able to charge the luxury on expenses. He shivered as the cab crawled down the Strand. The sky had that watery grey tinged with pink which often heralded snow. He shrank into his old herring-bone overcoat and contemplated the idiocy of his situation. He was too old at thirty-five for this sort of escapade. Would have been too old at twenty-five or even fifteen. Once more he was being forced to forsake the safe boring bowels of the Board of Trade for a masquerade. All because a boozy old journalist had been stabbed to death in his office. All because a mad newspaper proprietor had got the wrong end of the stick about his role in a previous case. All because newspaper proprietors have friends and influence. All because, years ago, Bognor had made a mistake about the course his life was to take. He glanced out at the Disney-Gothic of the Law Courts and the City's Coat of Arms in the middle of the road. It reminded him of reality. The City Police. They were in charge. He was superfluous. An embarrassment. It made his position doubly dangerous. Surplus to requirements, expendable—that would be the police view. A menace—that would be the murderer's view. He swore softly into the collar of his coat.

He had never visited the *Globe* office before. It was grotesque. The great pillars, the sweeping front steps and the 1930s gargoyles yielded to a marble hall dominated by a massive bust of Lord Wharfedale on a stone plinth. Each wall was covered in highly polished copper murals portraying, Bognor imagined, the virtues claimed by Lord Wharfedale on behalf of his newspapers. He noticed a beefy Achilles and a very old man with a quill pen who, he presumed, indicated wisdom. Above the entrance to the main staircase and lifts, in enormous purple lettering edged with gold, was the Wharfedale motto: 'The truth, the whole truth and nothing but the truth, so help me God.'

Bognor looked round to see if anyone could guide him to his Lordship's presence. A number of faintly grubby people were standing at lecterns reading old copies of the *Globe*. Others sat at two long tables, some in animated conversation. Behind a grill under the first two words of the truth slogan sat a man in a uniform and peaked cap. Bognor approached.

'I've come to see Lord Wharfedale.'

The official looked disbelieving. 'Have you filled in a form?'

'No.'

'You have to fill in a form. Then one of the reporters will deal with you.'

'I don't want to be dealt with by a reporter. I want to see Lord Wharfedale.'

'They all want to see Lord Wharfedale,' said the man sourly, 'I wouldn't mind seeing Lord Wharfedale myself.'

'I have an appointment.' Bognor produced an identity card and flashed it under the man's nose. It had the usual instant and desired effect.

'One moment please, sir.' He made a call on the internal phone. 'Mr Bognor to see Lord Wharfedale . . . right you are.' He turned back to Bognor. 'Take the lift to the tenth floor, and you'll be met.'

Bognor did as he was told. The lift was an antique contraption in mahogany and wrought iron which bore an inscription limiting its cargo to six adults. At least ten others crammed into it with Bognor. They all wore raincoats and smelt strongly of last night's alcohol. Mention was made of a football match the night before and they all got out on the third floor leaving him with a lonely passage through the next seven. At the tenth he got out and found himself transported into yet another world. The reception area here had carpet as thick as grass on a rugby pitch, soft lighting and a small fountain tinkling into a tiny pond. Waiting by the lift doors was a nubile blonde in a white canvas trouser suit.

'Mr Bognor?' she simpered, showing perfect teeth and dimples. 'Lord Wharfedale is waiting.' So saying she turned round and guided him through some yards of carpet, through a room in which three secretaries sat typing, through another which was empty except for a boardroom table and a dozen chairs and then paused before a heavy metal door which looked like the front of a safe. She pressed a buzzer and spoke into a grill to one side. In answer to her information the door moved to one side with a slight squeaking and Bognor was ushered into the presence.

Lord Wharfedale was short, podgy, sallow-complexioned and dressed in a three-piece suit of dark pin stripe set off by a vivid scarlet cravat secured with a pearl pin. He could have been any age over seventy-five.

'Mr Bognor,' he said coming round the desk, which was big as the boardroom table outside, and shaking hands. 'I've sent for you because of the way you handled the Beaubridge Friary affair. I thought it masterly. Masterly. Take your coat off. Sit down.'

Bognor did both and almost disappeared from view in the deep luxury of the brown leather upholstery.

'Cigar? Drink?' Bognor declined.

'You've heard of our murder?'

'Briefly.'

Lord Wharfedale took a cigar several sizes too big for him from a silver box and lit it with trembling fingers.

'What's your theory?'

'I don't know that I have enough to go on at this stage. What do the police think?'

Lord Wharfedale looked put out.

'I'm not overly impressed with the forensic abilities of our police force,' he said. 'The police have no officer class. This makes them stupid. Zealous they may be. Honest they may be. Intelligent they very rarely are. If I had my way the police would be recruited in the same fashion as the military. These other rank policemen should be confined to menial tasks. I want an intelligent gentleman to solve this business. That's why I sent for you.'

'I shall have to liaise with the police.'

'That's as maybe,' said Lord Wharfedale, tapping ash into a crystal bucket.

'What exactly do you want me to do?' asked Bognor, genuinely perplexed.

'Exactly what you did so admirably at Beaubridge Friary over the smuggled secrets. I want you to do what we in the newspaper industry call "get alongside" the situation. I want you to join the Samuel Pepys diary and read, mark, learn and inwardly digest all that goes on. Within the week if I'm any judge of character and ability in a man, and I am, we shall have our man ensnared.'

'I've no experience of journalism,' said Bognor feebly.

'That's as maybe. I had no experience of being a journalist before I became a journalist. Nor has anybody else. How many Prime Ministers have any experience of being Prime Minister before they become Prime Minister, eh? Answer me that.' Lord Wharfedale blew clouds of blue smoke about the room and appeared immoderately pleased by his own wisdom.

'Am I to say that I'm an investigator, or should I really pretend to be a journalist?'

'No pretence involved. You will be a journalist. I shall be paying you. As for saying that you're involved in investigative work that's up to you.' He pressed a red button on the desk and said in commanding tones,

'Send me Gringe.' Then he turned back to Bognor. 'Mr Gringe,' he said, 'was Mr Derby's deputy. Not an impressive specimen but loyal and conscientious. He will be in charge until we find a replacement.'

'Do you,' asked Bognor, greatly daring, 'have any theories about who might have killed Mr Derby?'

Lord Wharfedale inhaled and looked sagacious. 'St John Derby,' he said eventually, 'was a very remarkable man. He was the first war correspondent into Dachau. He covered the sinking of the *Tirpitz*. He once obtained an interview with Sir John Ellerman. Not a long interview. Not a very interesting interview. But an interview. They don't make them like St John Derby any more.'

'But you have no idea who might have killed him?'

'Why do people kill people? No point killing journalists. Most of them too busy committing suicide to make it worth the effort. You ever kill anyone?'

'No.'

'Not an easy thing to do. Not in cold blood. Have to be a hard man to stab someone to death with a paper knife.'

The buzzer buzzed and Mr Gringe was announced. Lord Wharfedale operated the door and introduced him.

'Gringe,' he said, waving his cigar, 'this young man is Simon Bognor who is joining your column on my personal instruction. He is to be treated with civility and to be assisted in whatever way he wishes. He will be invaluable to you. Mr Bognor, I will see you here at the same time next week to hear how you are progressing. Gringe, Mr Bognor here may not have a great deal of journalistic experience but he has flair. Flair, Gringe, flair. Important thing, flair. Would you recognize it if you saw it, Gringe? I wonder. Watch Mr Bognor, Gringe, and you will see flair at work. Encourage it. Foster it. Nurture it. One day perhaps you may develop the quality for yourself. And now good luck to you both, gentlemen. Oh, and Gringe, apart from the obituary for Mr Derby I shall be sending you a paragraph of my own for inclusion in the column. It will be with you at four. Good day to you both.'

Outside in the reception area Mr Gringe took a handkerchief from his breast pocket and mopped his brow which showed no sign of perspiration.

'I do find the proprietor intimidating,' he said, 'he's so brusque.' Bognor nodded. 'I should imagine they're all a bit like that, wouldn't you? Otherwise they wouldn't have got where they have.'

Mr Gringe nodded sadly. 'I suppose you're right,' he said, 'I just wish one's superiors were a little nicer.'

They got into the lift and pressed the button for the fifth floor.

'I'm afraid I don't know anything about your previous employment,' said Mr Gringe. 'Have you been with the group long?'

'About half an hour.'

'Oh,' he pursed his lips, 'which paper were you with before that?'

'Er . . .' Bognor thought of telling the truth and then decided against it. It would prove troublesome. Besides there was plenty of time for it to come out later. 'I spent a bit of time with the *Winnipeg Eagle*,' he said. 'But I'm not really a lifelong journalist. More a jack of all trades.'

'And how did you come to the notice of Lord Wharfedale?'

'Lord Wharfedale spreads his net very wide,' said Bognor elliptically and then noticed that Gringe was looking very censorious, not to say suspicious, not, indeed, to say disbelieving. 'My late father was a friend of his,' he said quickly. 'They knew each other in Capetown way back. And so when I found myself penniless and destitute I naturally wrote to him for a job. And here I am.'

They had arrived at the fifth floor and were walking along the path which the late St John Derby had taken to his death the night before. This floor, Bognor observed, merited a carpet, though not of the same prodigious depth as that on the tenth. Mr Gringe paused outside the Samuel Pepys office.

'Not a very South African name, Bognor?' he ventured.

'Well nor's Wharfedale come to that,' said Simon. 'we're Sussex actually. The Sussex Bognors . . . no?'

'No,' said Mr Gringe, distinctly icily, 'I think not.' He opened the door and showed him in.

It was, Bognor admitted, a comfortable office. It contrasted very favourably with his own dungeon at the Board of Trade. For a start there were windows, quite large ones, and although there wasn't what you might call a view to be obtained from them, and although it wasn't possible to see the sky from them, they still let in natural light. Most of the desks were arranged opposite each other against the walls, leaving the centre of the room free for movement, but one, which from the array of telephones on it and the mousey young woman behind it he judged to be the secretary's was just inside the door. Another, larger and more leathery than the rest, was separated from the main room by a glass screen. Its size and segregation proclaimed it a leader's desk and therefore almost certainly the property of the late St John Derby. The rest of the room was taken up with a standard assortment of wall maps, noticeboards with tasteful literate collages and graffiti, a colour television set and a Victorian umbrella stand. Ranged along the top of the bookcases, which contained such standard works of reference as *Whitaker, Who's Who, Wisden* and *Burke's Peerage* and on top of the filing cabinets were row upon row of empty champagne bottles. All this Bognor took in—if not at a glance at least in a fairly brisk gaze, but it was the people who interested him.

His arrival had clearly interrupted something. The inhabitants of the room were all frozen in mid-gesture, like characters in a film when the projector jams. The universal appearance of guilt and embarrassment made it quite clear that they had been discussing Mr Gringe. Mr Gringe, who looked as if he realized this and was far from flattered at the thought, turned flamingo pink and coughed.

'Er . . . Molly, um . . . gentlemen,' he said, 'this is our new colleague, Simon Bognor. He joins us today and does so . . .' here his voice assumed a grave portentousness, 'at Lord Wharfedale's personal instruction. He'll use my desk, since of course, well that is when we've moved some of Mr Albany's effects I shall naturally, well . . .'

Bognor stood and smiled inanely at no one in particular. It was Molly Mortimer who rescued the situation from its increasing ambiguity.

'Hi,' she said, holding out a hand which jangled with bangles and had long elegant fingers with long elegant painted nails. 'I'm Molly Mortimer, the ritual Samuel Pepys Lady. Every column has to have one to appease the women-in-media lobby. They'd much rather not of course.'

She was wearing a musky scent in such quantities that Bognor who had a poor nose for such things noticed and found it attractive. In a few years she would be over the hill, he thought, but just now she was in the middle of an Indian summer, somewhere around forty with good bones and no flab and just the right amount of make-up skilfully applied. The crisp white blouse was cotton but expensive, the scarlet skirt was a modest length but flared just enough to suggest excellent legs. Her auburn hair might have been helped with the bottle but not over much and her face showed enough lines to make it interesting in the right places, but not enough to do more than hint at a modicum of age or depravity. Bognor shook the hand with just the beginnings of enthusiasm.

'I'd better introduce the others,' she said, 'since Eric, poor darling, is so lacking in the conventional social graces. This,' she indicated a chubby degenerate in tweeds, 'is Milborn Port, or if the battle in which he has been engaged with the Pope to prove the legitimacy of his claim to the baronetcy is successful, *Sir* Milborn Port.'

'Everyone calls me Milly,' confided Mr Port, whose handshake was limp and clammy. 'Much easier than Milborn.'

'Milly and Molly,' said Simon facetiously, but no one even smiled. They had obviously heard it before.

'Bertie Harris,' continued Miss Mortimer, 'son and heir to the Wharfedale riches and for that matter the Wharfedale rags.'

Bognor looked at the lean handsome face and the tall elegant figure and tried to detect a family resemblance. Not easy. As so often with the sons of the extravagantly self-made Bertie had acquired a social manner which was quite at variance with his father's rough diamond behaviour. It was father's fault for having sent him to Eton and Trinity.

'How do you do?' asked Harris, expecting the answer 'How do you do?' and rolling the words into one.

'Howjado?' answered Bognor, coming dangerously close to parody. Harris noticed. Bognor noticed that he noticed, and worse still Harris noticed that Bognor had noticed that he'd noticed. Bognor gave himself a black mark and a silent reminder to be more tactful.

'Willy Wimbledon,' said Miss Mortimer. Bognor had heard of him, if only for his cricketing prowess. He had made a hundred before lunch in the Oxford and Cambridge match at Lord's the previous summer and had gone on to play some matches for Somerset. He was, unlike any of his colleagues, young, athletic and as yet unmarked by any of the awful things that happen to journalists after the age of twenty-one.

'Hi,' he said, flashing teeth without a trace of nicotine stain.

'Oh,' said Molly Mortimer, 'how dreadfully rude of me, I've forgotten our other ritual lady. Not so approved by the ladies of women's lib I'm afraid if only because she does all the work and gets none of the money. Without Anthea Morrison I'm afraid there simply wouldn't be a Samuel Pepys column, eh, Eric?'

Bognor smiled and nodded at the mousey young woman behind the desk near the door. She looked very young and slightly undistinguished to be ministering to such an obviously difficult and demanding collection of people, but there was something about her which warned him not to dismiss her too readily. She smiled and nodded back.

'I'm afraid,' said Eric Gringe, in an obvious effort to reassert his authority, 'that Horace Peckwater, the sub-editor who looks after us, won't be in until late afternoon. You'll have an opportunity to meet him then. Now let me show you your desk.' He bustled Bognor over to his desk and began to explain at great length where the stationery was kept, how to telephone to the library and find the gents. The others all went back to their own places where they read the morning papers or filled in expense claims. After about a quarter of an hour Milborn Port looked up from the *Morning Star*, coughed loudly, pulled out a fob watch, sighed and said to the room in general, 'I don't know about you chaps but I think in the circumstances I'm going to wander up the road. Anyone care to join me?'

There was a lot of muttering. Gringe said pointedly that he was too busy. Harris, equally pointedly, that it was too early. Miss Morrison was clearly too menial to be included in the invitation. Wimbledon and Miss Mortimer agreed.

'You coming, Simon?' asked Molly as she put on a heavy kangerooskin coat and an Hermes scarf.

'Um, where are you going?'

'El Vino, I should imagine. El Vino, Milly?'

'Yes, I think so.'

'OK,' said Bognor. It was a bit early for him too. Only just after half-past eleven but he had better, he argued, fit in with the folk lore of Fleet Street and in any case the day was exceptional.

'Not too long please,' said Gringe as they left, 'and not too much. There's still a column to produce.'

Outside in the corridor Molly and Willy giggled conspiratorially. 'Granny's being very grannyish today,' said Willy.

'It's death,' said Molly, 'makes him feel important.'

Outside in Fleet Street it was still bitterly cold and the grey light made what romantics and cynics called 'The Street of Adventure' look tawdry and even dull. True, the twin monoliths of the *Express* and the *Telegraph* opposite exuded a certain authority, the one raffish the other more solid and virtuous, but the rest of the newspaper offices belonged to the *Methodist Recorder* and the *Irish Independent* and a string of small provincial chains. Fleet Street itself had more cheap cafés and undistinguished pubs than national newspaper offices. *The Times*, the *Mail*, the *Sun*, the *Mirror* were all elsewhere. Only the *Globe* and the *Telegraph* and the *Express* with their satellites actually inhabited the street. Bognor felt a twinge of disappointment. He would have liked a street full of men in braces and green eye shades hurrying towards scoops of world shattering import. Instead he was beginning to have an impression of small men from Bromley with mortgages.

At least El Vino was different. As the four of them barged through the narrow door Bognor was assailed as he had been on previous occasions by the unmistakable aroma of spirit, wine and cigar fumes. No beer here and not so many cigarettes, at least of the English variety.

' 'Morning, Miss Mortimer, 'Morning, Mr Port, 'Morning, m'Lord,' said the stiff young man in the pin stripes and black coat behind the bar.

'Bottle of Pommery in the back please, Van,' said Mr Port as they passed through the dark passage-like room. They exchanged noisy greetings with another small group at a table. 'That's the Peterborough lot from the *Telegraph*,' said Miss Mortimer *sotto voce* as they found a table in the back, which had an air halfway between that of a gentleman's club and a railway waiting room. Already there were several drinkers crouched over bottles, mainly of champagne, though in some cases of claret or hock. Most of the men were elderly silver-haired individuals though at one table a group of younger men in striped shirts were drinking sweet sherry by the glass. 'Advertising men,' said Molly with disdain.

Bognor sat down in a revolving wooden chair with Lord Northcliffe's name carved in the back. Presently a girl arrived with four glasses and a bottle of Pommery and Greno champagne dripping with little beads of moisture. She poured some into a glass for Milborn Port who sipped and sniffed, pronounced it just right and gave her five pounds from which he took very little by way of change.

'Well,' said Molly Mortimer when all their glasses had been charged, 'what do *you* think, Milly?'

Mr Port started to look serious and then chuckled.

'Rather exciting, isn't it? I mean I'm sorry about the old boy but he'd had a good run and he was just about due for departure. Not a bad exit. I think we should drink a toast to absent friend. He'd appreciate it, and I suggest we should couple that with applause for the manner of his leaving us.'

'No but seriously,' said Molly, after they'd drunk, 'someone must have done it. But who?'

'I suppose the principal suspects are us,' said Willy Wimbledon flatly. The remark did not go down well.

'Oh really,' said Molly and Milly in unison.

Bognor disagreed. 'I think he has a point,' he said, 'and if not one of you then who else? Who else did he have dealings with?'

'Endless people,' said Milborn. 'You can't run something like the Pepys show without dealing with people.'

'His bookie,' said Molly.

'Bookie? Did he bet?'

'Regularly but lightly,' said Milborn, 'and he was a bookie's delight. Never won more than once or twice in a year. In any case he always put on with the shop over the road and I really don't see one of them pounding up to the office at midnight with a paper knife.'

'No.'

'What about his wife?' asked Bognor. '*Cherchez la femme* and all that.'

'You'll be accusing me next, darling,' said Molly, 'he hadn't seen Lotte for years and years. No reason to, there weren't any children and they had nothing in common.'

'Any more women, latterly I mean?' Bognor was suddenly aware that he was sounding a little eager. The other three seemed to sense something more than idle curiosity in his manner.

'I think it had been young men recently,' said Molly, 'I never much liked the way he looked at you, Willy. In fact I've always had my doubts about his hiring you in the first place. You have no qualifications whatever.'

'That makes two of us,' said Bognor brightly.

'Oh,' said Milborn. 'Where were you before exactly?'

Bognor decided to leave the fictitious *Winnipeg Eagle* out of his claims this time. 'I wasn't really anywhere actually,' he said, 'I'm afraid I've got in by the back door.'

There was a pause while they drank their champagne. Bognor noticed that Mr Port drank his faster than any of the rest of them. It was he who spoke next.

'Why do you say the principal suspects are us, Willy?' he asked. 'Rum sort of idea.'

The young man blushed a little.

'I think,' said Molly, 'he meant that the police are fearfully dim witted and will be hard pressed to think of anyone at all to suspect let alone accuse, and since the wretched man was done to death in our own office in the middle of a working week we are extremely convenient targets for the unimaginative mind.'

'There's slightly more to it than that,' said the Viscount. 'For a start whoever did it knew how to find the office without asking. If anyone had asked Albert the way he would remember.'

'Albert?' asked Bognor.

'The night porter,' said Milly. 'Go on.'

'Well secondly it looks as if it was probably someone he knew. Otherwise surely he'd have kicked up some sort of racket.'

'That doesn't follow,' said Molly, 'he was almost certainly too pissed to speak let alone make a racket.'

'Look at it another way,' said Wimbledon. 'Granny Gringe said he thought of us as his family which is a typically Granny-ish sort of thing to say but on the other hand it is quite accurate. He didn't have any real family and he didn't seem to have any real friends. Only acquaintances, and you surely don't get murdered by mere acquaintances?'

Milborn Port held up the now empty Pommery bottle and waved it in the direction of the waitress. Another arrived swiftly and Wimbledon and Molly Mortimer split the cost despite mumbled protestation from Bognor.

'You forget, darling,' said Molly, 'that unless you are a homicidal maniac which is a possibility that we can't rule out altogether, particularly in Fleet Street after the pubs have closed, then you need a motive for killing people and I don't see that any of us by any conceivable stretch of imagination could possible have a motive for killing St John.'

'Oh I don't know,' said Milborn, who had a reputation for becoming irritatingly arch under the influence of drink.

'You may need a motive but it can seem jolly flimsy to the outside eye. Knew a chap in the Gurkhas who killed someone because of BO.'

'BO?' Molly looked scandalized.

'Never washed under his arms or changed his socks and he had the next bed. Hacked him to death with a kukri. He got off.' He drank deeply and realized that he hadn't fully explained himself. 'There was a war on,' he said.

'I suppose Gringe had a motive,' said Wimbledon. 'He'd always wanted to run the column and St John obviously wasn't going to resign so perhaps he thought the only way to get the job for himself was to kill him.'

'Nonsense,' said Molly forcefully. 'Eric is one of nature's number twos and he knows it. Besides I don't believe he has the strength, let alone the nerve, to kill anyone with a knife. It's inconceivable.'

'There was a time, wasn't there, Molly, when you were on, shall I say rather closer terms with St John, than you had been recently?' Milborn, Bognor realized, was stirring. He judged that it was something he enjoyed doing.

'Oh really,' she said, 'you know bloody well that's a ridiculous thing to say. About fifteen years ago when I first joined the paper I occasionally went out to dinner with him, or once or twice to the theatre.'

'*I* understood you used to go to Paris for week-ends.'

'Oh for God's sake. We once met in Paris quite by accident when he was doing the *Prix de l'Arc de Triomphe* for the paper and I was stopping over after a holiday in St Trop. That was all. You men, you're all the same. Anyway what sort of motive does that give me? I'd hardly kill the old thing just because I went out with him once or twice in the dim and distant past. Would I? Be fair.'

She was very irritated. Bognor deflected attention.

'What about you Milborn?' he asked. 'Don't you have a motive?'

'What, me? No. I've never had a motive in my life. Totally impulsive I am. Nevertheless I dare say young Willy has one. Maybe Molly was right. Maybe St. John had been making improper advances, eh?'

Milborn, at least after a few drinks, was undoubtedly a mischief maker. On the other hand, Bognor conceded, Viscount Wimbledon was quite pretty enough to have excited the attention of an old pederast, if pederast he was.

'You know perfectly well,' he said, 'that my interests in sex are entirely conventional.'

'Precisely,' said Milborn. 'No doubt you found St John's attentions so distasteful that you felt compelled to knife him between the ribs.'

Bognor was beginning to find the conversation a strain.

'What we're all forgetting,' he said placidly, 'is that

in order to commit a crime you need opportunity as well as motive. If it turns out that you were all safely tucked up in bed in the small hours of this morning then it doesn't matter what sort of motive you might have had. If on the other hand you were rampaging about the city with no proper alibi then the absence of motive isn't going to impress the police. Once you've proved a murder it's suprising how easily a motive crops up just where no one was expecting it.'

'That lets me out anyway,' said Port. 'I went home early, had a few jars at the club and so to bed.'

'What time?'

'What time what?'

'Did you leave the club and go home?'

'About eleven. May be a bit earlier.'

'And got home when?'

'About ten minutes later. It's not far.'

'By car?'

'Yes.'

'Did anyone hear you come in?'

'My wife and I have separate rooms. I try not to wake her when I'm in late. She usually goes to bed early.'

'So even if she did wake she would be unlikely to notice the time?'

It was Milborn Port's turn to bridle. 'Look, exactly what are you getting at?'

'I'm simply trying to demonstrate the flimsiness of the average cast-iron alibi. Would she have noticed the time?'

'Probably not.'

'And where do you live?'

'Stoke Poges.'

'And what sort of car do you drive?'

'Jaguar. Second hand.'

'Well there you are then.'

'Where?'

Molly Mortimer laughed a little too humourlessly. 'In the dock in a second, Milborn darling. What Simon has just proved, rather adroitly if I may say so, is that it would have been perfectly possible for you to drive from your club—golf club I take it—straight to the *Globe*, carry out the dastardly deed and drive home to bed without your wife suspecting anything. In other words your alibi's collapsed.'

'That's ridiculous. I was devoted to the old boy.'

'That's not the point,' said Viscount Wimbledon, 'nobody's saying you did it. All Simon's proved is that you had the opportunity to do it.'

'Bloody silly if you ask me,' said Milborn, pouring himself another glass and ostentatiously neglecting the others. At which disintegrating point in the meeting they were saved by the bell.

'Telephone call for Mr Port,' said the waitress breathlessly.

'No need to ask what that's about,' he said. 'Granny Gringe calling for her straying flock.' He hurried to the telephone which was near the front door, while the others finished their drinks.

'That was very naughty, Simon,' said Molly. 'He didn't enjoy it.'

3

The recall to the *Globe* was not prompted just by Eric Gringe's understandable wish to get some work done. The law had arrived and was conducting formal questioning in an office on the third floor which had been kindly vacated by the leader writer in charge of Mediterranean affairs, the Liberal Party and cricket. This sort of random specialization was based on Lord Wharfedale's famous maxim that 'Half measures often make a whole truth' and also on his no less celebrated aphorism that 'Too much knowledge is as dangerous as too little.' In consequence many of the *Globe*'s writers were encouraged not to specialize in one subject to the exclusion of all others as happened on some papers,

nor to be 'general reporters' who could turn their hand
to anything. Instead *Globe* men tended to be moderately well informed on a few subjects. The leader
writer in question had been delighted for an excuse to
leave the building and was even now heading towards a
Mediterranean affair at the Italian Tourist Office.

Mr Gringe, Bertie Harris and the secretary, Anthea
Morrison, had already been questioned by the police
and they now wanted a word with Milborn Port who
dutifully shambled off downstairs. After he had done
so Mr Gringe took Bognor on one side.

'I'm afraid we've had trouble,' he said, sotto voce.

'Trouble?'

'It's the chapel. I was afraid we'd have trouble with
the chapel the minute you said your experience was so
limited. We had enough trouble with Lord Wimbledon
and we only got him in because they promised it would
be the last time it was allowed to happen.'

'I'm sorry, I'm not with you. What has chapel got to
do with anything?'

Mr Gringe sighed. 'You're not a member of the
Union, are you?'

'No, but Lord Wharfedale . . .'

'Oh dear,' Mr Gringe looked painfully distressed.
'I'm afraid you're going to find this quite unlike the
Winnipeg Eagle. The time when Lord Wharfedale had
the absolute right of hire and fire has passed for ever.
If the chapel doesn't approve then you can't work
here.'

'The chapel's the Union branch?'

Mr Gringe came as near withering Bognor as his essentially cowardly appearance allowed. 'Where on
earth have you been all this time?'

'Winnipeg,' said Bognor, 'I told you. In Winnipeg it
was called a branch not a chapel.'

'And were you a member?'

'No.'

Mr Gringe sighed again. 'I'm afraid,' he said, 'that
this is going to turn out to be one of those days. We

have to go and see the Father of the Chapel . . . the Branch secretary that is.'

'I'd no idea the language of journalism was so archaic,' said Bognor.

Together they left the Pepys office and took the lift to the third floor, from which they passed through a set of swing doors narrowly avoiding a collision with a large man in carpet slippers who had a long-extinguished cigar end clenched between his teeth. Mr Gringe apologized effusively for the near miss and called him 'Sir' twice. The man appeared much mollified and said something which the cigar end rendered inaudible.

The room in which they now found themselves was as vast as an aeroplane hangar and contained, Bognor guessed, about a hundred people. All of them were in shirtsleeves except for a very occasional female who seemed overdressed in such sweaty surroundings. Most of the men sat at long benches, some of them in front of huge primitive typewriters connected to the desks by heavy chains.

Overhead strips of neon illuminated a variety of appropriate slogans painted on hoardings. Apart from the Wharfedale Truth adage Bognor noticed 'Make it fast, make it accurate,' 'Don't make it up, make it true,' and 'Late copy costs money.' It was very noisy. Some men were pounding at the typewriters which looked as if they had been fashioned from wrought iron and made a correspondingly clanging din, others were reading bits of paper with woebegone expressions and cursing from time to time, one or two were haranguing telephone receivers with such enthusiasm that the phones seemed superfluous. Ticker tape machines coughed out news from the agencies, conferences were taking place in small glass booths and a stout lady was dispensing tea from a chipped enamel pot on a trolley. Bognor stopped briefly to read a brief notice headed 'Bulletin' and signed 'Editor'. It said 'Congratulations to all staff on the brilliant handling of the Welsh colliery disaster which completely floored the opposition. A pity this was marred by the poor treatment of the MacGregor Quins.' Underneath another again signed by the Editor reminded him of his responsibilities. 'It is with much regret that I announce the death of St John Derby, Editor of the Samuel Pepys column. There will be a private funeral. Details of a memorial service will be announced later.'

'Come along, Mr Bognor, please, we haven't got all day and there is a column to produce. You have to be at the Dorchester by twelve-thirty.' It was the first Bognor had heard of this but he said nothing. Mr Gringe led the way across the room to a far corner where a thin, ginger-haired man in maroon braces was sucking a pipe and sticking pieces of paper on a spike.

'Simon,' said Mr Gringe, 'this is Alastair Tweedie, the Chief Assistant to the Deputy Foreign Copytaster and Father of the Chapel. Father, this is Mr Bognor about whom you were enquiring.'

The Chief Assistant to the Deputy Foreign Copytaster removed the pipe for a moment and regarded Bognor with unconcealed malevolence.

'Aye,' he said in nasal Glaswegian, 'this is a right how do you do and no mistake.'

Bognor shuffled his feet.

'In what sense?'

The sour-faced Scot paid no attention.

'You're not a member of the National Union of Journalists.'

'No, but . . .'

'No "buts", sonny. I don't suppose you've earned the major proportion of your income from journalistic activities for the last three years either?'

'Well . . .'

'Well nothing. Yes or No. I don't have all day.'

Bognor guessed that that was precisely what he had.

'Well I was hired personally by Lord Wharfedale and since this is his paper I rather imagined . . .'

'Bugger Lord Wharfedale. As far as I'm concerned this newspaper is the property of those who work for

it, and I'm not having anybody working for it who isn't
in the Union and that's all there is to it.'

He got to his feet. 'If Lord Wharfedale doesn't
concede on this I'm calling a mandatory meeting this
afternoon,' he said to Gringe. 'We'd better tell Bert
Watson and you'd better come too. Both of you. That
man will kill this paper if he goes on like this.'

So saying he led the way through another pair of
swing doors at the rear of the room, down a flight of
stairs through another immense aeroplane hangar full
of silent machines and along a passage to a door labelled, to Bognor's incredulity, 'Imperial Father'.

Quite involuntarily he found himself singing softly,
'Imperial Father, strong to save, whose hand hath
stilled the restless wave.' His companions looked at
him, scandalized, and Mr Tweedie knocked twice on
the Imperial Father's door.

Inside the two fathers greeted one another.

' 'Morning, Father.'

' 'Morning, Father.'

Mr Watson was a heavily-jowled fifty-year-old with
little piggy eyes and an air of enormous self-impor-
tance.

Mr Gringe, who evidently cut no ice with either of
these important men, was introduced formally and
Bognor, grudgingly. Mr Watson spoke in the slight
whine of south London.

'You've ascertained that the essential facts are as
you suspected,' he said.

'Aye.'

'Well, Bognor, do you have any mitigating circum-
stance to suggest why you should take work from a
professional trade union member who should by rights
have the job you've been given?'

'Yes.' Bognor was put out, not by the trade union-
ism of which he approved in principle, but by the turgid bureaucracy of it all.

'I've told him it's no good taking Lord Wharfedale's
name,' said Tweedie, waving his pipe, 'if that's what
he's going to do.'

'As a matter of fact no,' said Bognor. 'Something quite different but I'm not prepared to discuss it in front of a third party. It's a matter for the Imperial Father as senior Union official in the organization and for him alone.' He watched the self-satisfied beginnings of a smile on Mr Watson's face and realized that he had judged his man correctly.

'If you have something to say you can say it to me,' said Tweedie.

'Sorry,' said Bognor, 'Imperial Father or no one.'

'In that case,' said Tweedie, 'it'll have to be no one and it's the responsibility of you and Lord Wharfedale if there's no paper tomorrow.'

'I'm not so certain, Father,' said Mr Watson ponderously, 'but in the present parlous state of our industry one may be advised to behave sometimes in a manner which may seem unconstitutional. If you and Mr Gringe would leave this to me it shouldn't take a moment. I'm aware that it's strictly out of order but these are difficult times.'

It was not a popular decision but the Imperial Father outranked the others. Mr Gringe left happily enough, Mr Tweedie made it clear that he did so under duress.

'Now, Mr Bognor,' said Mr Watson when they'd gone, 'it had better be good. I'm a busy man.'

'Like hell,' he thought, producing the identity card which usually had such an immediate and dramatic effect. The Imperial Father read through it twice, then looked up.

'I'm glad you told me about this,' he said in a slow almost sepulchral voice clearly intended to demonstrate that he understood the momentousness of the confidence Bognor had imparted, 'although it would have saved a great deal of embarrassment if his Lordship had confided in me at the very start. I take it you've been "planted" to investigate Mr Derby's sad death.'

Bognor thought of congratulating him on his quick-witted perspicacity and then thought better of it. 'Yes,' he said, 'I think it would be best if as few people as possible knew about it.'

'I quite understand, perfectly. I can guarantee to prevent any trouble for a week. After that I'm afraid I may have problems with some of my colleagues. Mr Tweedie, for instance, is a very conscientious member of the Trade Union Movement.' He went to the door, opened it and readmitted Messrs Tweedie and Gringe. They came in and sat down on the stiff dining-room chairs which were all that the Imperial Father boasted apart from the upholstered high back chair he used himself.

'Gentlemen,' he said, 'I've listened to what Mr Bognor has told me and after due deliberation and taking cognizance of all the available facts in a special situation I have decided to grant him a probationary week provided steps are put in motion to ensure that his application for Union membership goes forward forthwith.'

Mr Tweedie was not amused. 'With respect, Father,' he remonstrated, making disgusting saliva based noises with his pipe, 'he can't be a member of the Union with his lack of experience. At the very least he has to go to Manchester.' Bognor shuddered.

'There are special circumstances, Father,' said Mr Watson.

'Then I have a right to know what they are.'

'It is within my discretion to decide otherwise. In my view the circumstances are sufficiently special to warrant special behaviour. A probationary week gentlemen . . . er, Mr Bognor would you stay a moment?'

'Just two things, Mr Bognor.' Bognor guessed there was never just one thing. Mr Watson was the sort of man who spoke in catalogues.

'The Pepys column, Mr Bognor, I think I ought to warn you about it. It's a peculiar place. You see they're not really journalists and it's not really journalism to my way of thinking. The only one of them who would ever hold down a job in the news room is that Gringe and there are those on the paper who still say he can't tell his arse from his elbow. But the rest of them . . . I'm not a killjoy, Mr Bognor, and I'll buy my round with the best of them *and* I'll have a bet when it suits me. The drinking and the gambling and, they say drugs, not to mention the sexual behaviour that goes on in that office. It's a scandal. Always has been. I'm surprised there's been no murder there before. Each one of them at the other's throats. You can hear them at it sometimes. Hysterical shouting, swearing, screaming. It's been a job to get a secretary to stay there at all until Miss Morrison arrived and the young man who was there before Lord Wimbledon had to leave. They found him in the wastepaper basket covered in ink and treacle.'

Bognor looked incredulous. 'Ink and treacle?'

'You may not credit it but it's true. The matter wasn't pursued. No one ever found out what really happened.'

'Sounds like school.'

'Well I'm warning you, it's a peculiar place. The second thing is Miss Morrison. She's a sensible lass is Miss Morrison. Not a member of the National Union of Journalists you understand, she belongs to SOGAT.'

Bognor recognized the initials of one of the printers' unions of which he guessed Mr Watson was a leading light.

'We've found her a very reliable source of information in the past, Mr Bognor, I'll say no more than that. The rest of them treat her as if she were a Hottentot. Talk in front of her as if she wasn't there. She knows more about that office than any of the so-called journalists in it. I'll tip her the wink and then she'll be invaluable to you.'

'I'd rather you didn't let on that I was, well, that I was here in an investigative capacity.'

'I can be as discreet as the next man,' said Mr Watson, 'and I will be. I'll wish you the best of luck.' He held out a fat hairy hand and screwed up his piggy eyes. 'The truth, the whole truth and nothing but the truth, so help me God, eh?' he said and laughed.

Upstairs Mr Gringe was floundering among papers. No one else was there except Miss Morrison who was fighting a defensive battle on the telephone. 'No, I'm sorry, Mr Pepys is in conference . . . certainly I'll pass on your idea . . . yes I agree Northamptonshire butterflies are extremely important.'

Mr Gringe looked at Bognor with grave suspicion. 'What did you say to the Imperial Father? I don't imagine you told him about your experiences on the *Winnipeg Eagle*. Tweedie is far from satisfied. Indeed I fear that if he has his way there will still be some form of industrial action before the week is out.'

Bognor shrugged and smiled. 'I thought the Imperial Father was very reasonable,' he said. 'He just thought I should be given a chance.'

'Yes, well.' Mr Gringe picked up a small pile of papers from a corner of the desk. 'I wonder if you'd be good enough to have a go at these. You know the style. Not more than one hundred and fifty words at the very most, preferably a hundred. Six copies of each piece you write. Name of informant at the top where appropriate, plus of course your own name which is, ha, always appropriate, and not too many adjectives. The sentences can be as long as you like—not like the *Express*—but please try to make the paragraphs short. Lord Wharfedale hates long paragraphs. Oh and the policeman wants to see you in Room 312 on the third floor and before you go Anthea will give you the invitation to the British Food Manufacturers Federation at the Dorchester. That should make rather a good tale. The Minister's speaking. See you after lunch.'

Bognor felt battered. He stuffed the pieces of paper into his coat pocket and scrutinized the invitation which said, 'The British Food Manufacturers requests the pleasure of the company of Mr S. Pepys at luncheon.' It would be interesting to know how many British Food Manufacturers thought that Samuel Pepys was alive and well and living in Fleet Street. He was not looking forward to the interview with the policeman. The more he thought about it the more intolerable the interference became. St John Derby's death was murder pure and if not simple at least not complicated by those considerations of industrial espionage which were the usual pretext for intervention by Bognor's department. If he were the detective in charge of the investigation he would be harassed enough already without the added bother of what in this instance amounted to a private detective ferreting around in a feeble disguise.

So it was a pleasant surprise to find that the temporary occupant of Room 312 was quite affable. He was not much older than Bognor, thinner, more sprightly and a lot more intelligent looking than Lord Wharfedale's prejudices would admit.

'Hi,' he said. 'My commiserations. I can't imagine you're wildly amused to be playing charades with this mob.'

'Not actually,' said Bognor. 'It wasn't my idea.'

'I'm aware of that, anyway my name is Graham Sanders.'

'Bognor,' said Bognor.

'Yes.' Sanders was smoking Embassy tipped. He offered one to Bognor, who declined, then lit another. Bognor noticed that the ash tray was already almost full. 'I've taken a whole lot of statements,' said the policeman, 'which frankly is a pretty fatuous exercise, and the carpet is being analysed although it's perfectly obvious that they'll find nothing more than a mixture of three parts blood to two parts port, and they're doing the paper knife for prints. None of which is going to help. Do you have any theories?'

'Not very hard ones,' said Bognor, relieved at his colleague's breeziness. 'I take it you think it's someone on the column?'

'Christ knows,' said Sanders, 'it seems the most likely, but the whole business is so improbable that I'd believe anything.'

'What were the statements like?'

'If you believed them then they were all safely tucked up in bed by midnight at the latest—the Mortimer woman and the Wimbledon boy together by the way.'

'I rather imagined that.'

'She claimed they ran into each other at "Hell's Own Angel" by chance and went home for a nightcap. He says they agreed to have dinner and then he missed the last bus. It doesn't matter which one's true. I get the impression she's had every other member of the staff at some time or another. You'd better watch out. You'll probably be next.'

Bognor laughed. 'Anything else? I've got to rush off to some ghastly binge at the Dorchester.'

'Poor old you! No nothing yet,' he paused, 'except this. It may be just a doodle, I don't know. I don't recognize it but I suppose it might just have some significance.' He passed over a scrap of paper torn from a loose leaf note book. Bognor read it:

In the city set upon slime and loam
They cry in their parliament 'Who goes home?'.

'Funny,' he said, 'I don't think I've read that before. My guess is that it's Chesterton, but that's only a hunch.'

'Based on what?'

Bognor laughed. 'I'd like to pretend it's based on rhyme, metre, sentence construction, language but it's just that when I was briefed on Derby I was told he was something of an authority on Chesteron. Apparently he could quote great chunks of the stuff.'

'I've never read any Chesterton,' said Sanders.

'You haven't missed much. If you leave it with me I'll try and check it out. My girl friend's passable at Chesterton and Belloc. I'll get her to do some research. Now I must go to this bloody thing at the Dorchester.'

He was late at the Dorchester. Yet again he had taken a taxi and it had crawled along Piccadilly and up Park Lane so slowly that he kept on being passed by pedestrians. After a bit it became a game. He would pass a walker as the cab put on a spurt only to be overtaken once more as he was halted at a traffic light. He helped to while away the time by examining the bits of paper that Gringe had given him. The first was from the Public Relations Officer of the Prince of Wales Own Midland Light Infantry, announcing that the Regiment had been granted the freedom of Walsall and would march through the town with fixed bayonets and bugling bugles the following Saturday. The regimental mascot, a Hereford Bull called Charlie, would also be participating. Across the top Gringe had written. 'Excellent as is. No need to change except delete adjectives.' Bognor could find very few adjectives indeed except for 'brown' in front of bull. He wondered if he was supposed to delete the 'Midland' and 'Light' in front of Infantry. The second was a handwritten letter from a Cheltenham address asking for support for the hundredth anniversary celebrations of the Gloster Thespians, an amateur theatrical society of which the writer was evidently patron. On this Gringe had written, 'Friend of Lord Wharfedale's, so regard as a must. Please telephone for further facts.' The third was typed on headed paper which proclaimed Duncan Andrews, freelance journalist, London and new York, and, in red typing, 'This is original, exclusive to the Samuel Pepys column and needs no checking.' Underneath there were just two sentences. 'I understand that the Countess of Cornwall, the former dancer and variety artiste Chloe Chicago, recently had a baby daughter at Queen Charlotte's maternity hospital. The Countess, who is separated from her husband, has recently been seen around London nightspots with Archie de la Rochefoucauld, the drummer.' On this Gringe had pencilled, 'Lord Wharfedale is very keen on this sort of thing, but you will obviously have to ring Queen Charlotte's to see if it is true.' He had just read the final item which was 'Seen outside South London church: "Swap tedium for Te Deum".' when he finally arrived at the Dorchester. Across the Te Deum joke Gringe had written, 'Please check and retype' and Bognor had a terrible vision of being required to tramp round every church in South London. Christ, he thought, if these were the sort of demands Derby was making no wonder he was bumped off. He wondered how much longer, on that basis, Gringe had got.

Inside the hotel he quickly established that the private room in which the Food makers were lunching was down a passage to the right. Despite the time which was almost forty minutes after the scheduled kick-off, guests were still drinking in the bar. He asked for a dry martini and wrinkled his nose when the waiter produced just that. He must remind himself to ask for 'dry martini cocktail' otherwise he was bound to get vile neat vermouth. On an easel in the corner there was a seating plan which he managed to consult just as the toastmaster, in a scarlet coat two sizes too small, boomed out 'My Lords, Ladies and Gentlemen, luncheon is served.' The Food makers obviously believed in keeping the press away from normal people. They were all at a separate table and Bognor saw that S. Pepys, *Daily Globe,* was sandwiched between J. Evelyn, *Evening Clarion*, and Parson Woodforde of the *Sunday News*. Looking round he half expected to see gentlemen in wigs and frock coats but was relieved to find that the uniform of the day was exactly what he was wearing—a shiny two piece grey worsted that had known better days.

John Evelyn of the *Clarion* turned out to be a spotty individual called Clough who had only recently joined after two years general reporting for a paper on the Isle of Wight, while Parson Woodforde was an older version of the same thing with a row of biro's neatly arranged in his jacket pocket and a light fall of dandruff on his shoulders. Lunch, or luncheon consisted of sole in a white sauce, lamb and an ice cream concoction with pineapple. Bognor, however, had little time to notice this since his neighbours started bombarding him the minute grace had been said.

'You're new, aren't you?'

'What actually happened to old Derby then?'

'Don't tell me it was a stroke. That's not what they're saying in El Vino.'

'Pull the other one.'

'If you ask me it was pretty Lord Wimbledon, fed up with being touched up in the office.'

'I should think the *Globe*'s glad to see the last of him. He'd been useless the last five years—always spouting poetry, or playing bridge at his club or watching cricket at the Oval. He hadn't done a hand's turn for years. Bloody awful column too.'

'Maybe it was Lord Wharfedale himself then. I don't suppose the Union would let him sack the old bugger.'

'What's the chat in the office anyway?'

'I suppose it wasn't suicide?'

' 'Course that Milborn Port's a funny guy. Vicious tempered if you brush him up the wrong way.'

'Then there's always Molly—didn't he have an affair with her, way back?'

'Everyone's had an affair with Molly Mortimer. They don't call her the office bicycle for nothing.'

'Ha! Ha! Ha!'

'Ha! Ha! Ha!'

'Bloody good nosh at the Dorchester.'

'Couldn't have been the sub, could it?'

'I don't know. Not the sort of thing a sub would do, is it? Too busy butchering the copy to butcher one of the writers.'

'Ha! Ha! Ha!'

'What about Bertie Harris then?'

'What about Bertie Harris? Not him, he's too toffee nosed for anything like that. Wouldn't soil his hands with knocking people off in the office.'

'Isn't that him over there?'

'Where?'

'Over there. Sitting next to Miss Natural Yoghurt, the one with the cleavage and the big tits.'

'Don't fancy her.'

'No but is it Harris?'

For the first time Bognor was interested. Not,

naturally, in the beauty queen's breasts but in the possible presence of Lord Wharfedale's heir.

He craned his neck to get a view of the top table and met the gaze of Miss Natural Yoghurt across the room. She blushed.

'Come on, old boy, restrain yourself,' said his older neighbour.

'It *is* Bertie Harris,' said Bognor. 'I wonder what he's doing here?'

'Old Wharfedale's got a dairy farm somewhere in Rutland, hasn't he?' said Parson Woodforde.

'Wins prizes,' said John Evelyn.

'It's a bit thick,' said Bognor. 'I mean he might have said he was coming. It's ridiculous having two of us here. I hope he's going to write the story.'

'What are you griping for? It's a free meal, isn't it?'

' 'Course he won't write the story. Like I said he's not going to get his paws mucky doing anything like your actual work. He doesn't do any more work than old Derby did. Idle sod.'

'Bloody privilege. Almost makes you into a socialist, dunnit?' said the younger of the two journalists taking a gulp of Niersteiner. 'He's always playing polo with your lot, isn't he?'

'With Macarthy,' said the man from the *News*. 'They were at Oxford together. Poor little rich boys waiting for their fathers to kick the bucket. Look at him.'

All three turned to stare at Bertie who was deep in conversation with the woman on the opposite side to the beauty queen. She was tweedy and plain but looked, unlike her nubile rival, as if she could string a couple of sentences together.

'Bloody silly having people like him poncing around pretending to be journalists. Bet he's never done a doorstep in the middle of winter.'

'I'd like to see him have a go at some bloody court reporting. You going on this Liberace do this afternoon?'

'Do you reckon there'll be any booze?'

'It's at tea time.'

'Shouldn't make any bloody difference.'

'Are you going?' they asked Bognor. He sighed inwardly and attempted to make conversation. He did not find it easy.

Mercifully the speeches arrived early. The loyal toast had been proposed before the ice cream so that gentlemen could smoke. Passable cigars were circulated and Bognor settled down behind one, prepared to go quietly to sleep. Already he had had about half a bottle of champagne, some vermouth, a fair amount of hock and now a generous brandy. It was enough to make anyone sleepy, as was the Federation's president, Lord Netherweather. His Lordship, who farmed most of Dorset and Wiltshire, knew a great deal about subsidies and milk yields, harrows and marrows, and silage and combine harvesters. He had not, however, mastered after dinner speaking. Bognor was gently dreaming about paper knives and port when he was nudged sharply by John Evelyn. To his amazement he saw that every other person at the table was taking a shorthand note of Lord Netherweather's words. He was berating the Common Market agricultural policy and the medieval methods of the French peasantry. Bognor had no notebook. He took out the bits of paper that Gringe had given him and wrote down some words as fast as he could. After a few minutes he had written 'Extremely silly, nay mendacious—seven and three-quarter per cent—butter mountain—Johnny Onion men on bicycles (laughter).' It made no more sense than Lord Netherweather. He looked at his colleague Bertie Harris and saw, as he had feared, that he was sitting with his arms folded across his chest and his eyes fixed firmly on Miss Natural Yoghurt's ample, heaving bosom. Bognor was not amused. After what seemed an age the Minister stood up. He was crisp. Beginning with the joke about the Texan who boasted that it took two days to drive round his ranch and the Devonian who replied that he had a car like that too, he used it to defend the principle of the good little 'un being better than the bad big 'un, adding that the bigger they come the harder they fall. He assured his listeners that the Government were doing all in their power to make the Common Market work for the benefit of the British Farmer who was the best (cheers), most efficient (cheers) and above all most hard working (cheers) and cheerful (cheers) in the world. Whereupon, without more ado it gave him very great pleasure to present the first British Food Federation Award for Outstanding Services to British Food, to Lord Wharfedale.

This award was made in recognition of his Lordship's magnificent work on behalf of the industry, not only as a food producer himself—and he thought it would offend no one if he said here and now that Lord Wharfedale's farm at Wolding St Frideswide was without question the finest of its kind anywhere in the world—but also because of the truly remarkable campaign of support and encouragement which he had waged through the columns of his great newspapers with which although he had to confess he did not always see eye to eye on everything (laughter) he always agreed when it came to matters agricultural. It was a great sadness to him that Lord Wharfedale was unable to be here to take advantage of this delicious lunch and to accept this absolutely magnificent trophy, but nevertheless he was absolutely delighted that the Hon Robert Harris, Lord Wharfedale's son and heir, who was himself a countryman to his fingertips—green fingertips you could say (more laughter)—and who was of course also closely involved in the running of Wharfedale newspapers was here to accept on his father's behalf. And so without more ado he would hand it over.

The award appeared to take the press by surprise. No mention of it had been made among the sheaves of paper with which they had been provided. At least it explained Harris's presence. He took the prize, which was a silver cow, being milked by a silver milkmaid on a silver stool and made a very brief apology of a speech. 'I'm exceedingly pleased to accept this truly magnificent prize from you, sir, on behalf of my Father and I really feel it would be impertinent of me to add further to the words of wisdom we have heard already. I only hope that our future deeds will continue to find as much favour with you in the years to come and I promise you that some account of today's proceedings will appear in tomorrow's Samuel Pepys column of the *Daily Globe*, price three pence. Thank you all very much.' There followed much laughter and applause in which the journalists pointedly refused to join.

Immediately afterwards the party broke up. Bognor's lunching companions announced their intention of going in search of more drink and Liberace while he himself riffled through his notes wondering whether he was seriously expected to write a story about such odd goings on when he felt a hand on his shoulder. Turning round sharply he nearly collided with the silver milking scene which Betrie Harris was holding rather sheepishly under one arm.

'I didn't realize you were coming,' he said. 'I told Derby the other day that I'd write a note myself but I suppose in the confusion . . .' he cleared his throat. 'Well, it can't be helped. I hope your lunch was agreeable. I thought the food was perfectly bloody.'

Bognor said his food had been perfectly agreeable but that the company had been poor. 'I do wish they wouldn't always put us at the press table,' said Harris, 'I mean we're *not* press. Not *that* sort of press. And how they expect you to pick up any stories of the slightest interest sitting with that sort of person God alone knows.'

'Miss Natural Yoghurt didn't look exactly scintillating.'

Bertie wrinkled his nose. 'Silly girl,' he said, 'but perfectly agreeable in a bovine sort of way. I have my car outside would you care for a lift? If you're going back to the office that is.'

Bognor accepted. Even on the expense allowance he was confidently expecting the thought of another taxi had been filling him with apprehension. On the other hand he had to get back fairly soon if he was to make a shot at writing some stories.

'Will you really write that story?' he asked Harris as they walked towards the parking meter where the car had been left.

'Story?' he asked.

'About your father's award and the lunch and everything.'

'Oh Lord yes, I'll knock some old rubbish out. No problem. Don't worry. I expect you've got quite enough on your plate already.' Bognor thought of the curious pieces of paper in his jacket and blanched. 'Yes,' he said, 'to be precise I have the Gloster Thespians, the Prince of Wales Own Midland Light Infantry, and an illegitimate child of the Countess of Cornwall.'

Harris chuckled. 'That's not quite what I meant,' he said.

The car had a parking ticket on the windscreen when they found it and Harris tore it in half disdainfully and threw it in the gutter. 'Fancy a quick Krug,' he asked, 'to remove the taste of lunch?'

'Er . . .' Bognor in the ritual reflex of the middle class Englishman invited to take alcohol outside pub hours, glanced at his watch.

Harris noticed and laughed again. 'Easy to see you're not a journalist,' he said. 'Don't worry it's not long after three and there are plenty of places less inhibited than El Vino or the Coach and Horses.' The car was a Cambridge blue Porsche and despite the heavy traffic and the ponderous and prolific pedestrians they were in Soho within ten minutes. Harris parked ostentatiously on a double yellow line and led the way down a dark passage, up a dark flight of stairs and into a dark room where half a dozen men and a single woman sat furtively, talking in low guilty voices. Harris ordered a whole bottle of Krug, paid with a ten-pound note and carried it to a table far away from the bar and at least ten yards from the nearest potential eavesdropper.

'I thought,' he said, offering Bognor a Turkish cigarette from a packet marked 'Sullivan and Powell', 'that it might be a good idea to have a chat.'

'By all means,' said Bognor, thinking that if he had much more to drink he was going to start falling over.

'Have you got anywhere?'

'Not really, it's always difficult when you're suddenly moved into a completely strange organization. It takes time to adjust.'

'I really meant, do you have any ideas about the murderer?'

'Ah.' Bognor had forgotten temporarily that this was Lord Wharfedale's son. 'You mean you know who I am?'

Bertie Harris looked at him in a way which through the gloom and the alcohol Bognor judged to be quizzical.

'Naturally,' he said. 'After all I am my father's son.'

'That doesn't follow.'

'I'm sorry, I'm not quite with you.'

'I mean it doesn't follow that because you're your father's son you know everything that he does.'

'Well in this case, actually, it does.' Harris blew Turkish smoke elegantly through flared nostrils and tapped ash on to the carpet. 'He's not young and I shall take over in due course and it's therefore essential that I should be kept in touch with the running of the organization.'

'They why are you employed on the Samuel Pepys column?'

He sighed. 'My father and I agreed that I should spend as much time as possible learning how the paper functions. So I've worked in the city office, I've been in Washington, Beirut and Paris, I've had a spell in management and I've even worked in the accounts department God help me. Now I'm having a look at the diary. After all some people think it's the most important part of the paper. The fact that you and I, I suspect, think it's utter drivel is neither here nor there. I *am* also on the board—a fact which some people forget, stupidly I always think.'

'I see.' Bognor didn't really see, but he was damned if he was going to say so.

'Anyway,' Bertie continued, pouring more Krug, 'I can probably help you out with some background material which otherwise would be hard to come by. For starters, you know why my father is so particularly anxious to have the business cleared up.'

'Not apart from the obvious reasons. I suppose there are some un-obvious reasons.'

'Of a sort. You see, St John Derby, despite his glorious past, was a dreadful old lush and no use to man or beast for the past five years at least. My father wanted to pension him off, which was absolutely the right thing to do, but the Union wouldn't have it.'

'The Union seems to be very strong at the *Globe*.'

'It's the same everywhere. They're killing the industry. My view is that one should stand up to them. Show them who's boss. If you got rid of a few of the ringleaders the rest would come round pretty quickly. We treat our chaps extremely well. For instance I don't know if you know but every single one of our employees' families gets a Christmas box. Some people say that's paternalism. I say it's thoughtfulness. However we're getting off the point. My father had had several chats with St John asking him to leave, but the old boy just dug his heels in and refused to budge. So naturally you'll understand that my father felt extremely—shall we say peculiar—when this happened.'

'You're not suggesting,' alcohol had robbed Bognor of any tact he might ordinarily possess, 'that your father arranged it?'

Harris seemed genuinely surprised, though not particularly shocked.

'Good Lord no,' he said. 'That's most unlikely. Well, pretty unlikely. Or put it another way, if my father had arranged anything like that,' and he suddenly seemed to become extremely serious, 'then it would have been a thoroughly professional job. No messing around with paper knives in the dead of night. He'd probably have been, oh I don't know, run over by one of the vans I should think. That's always happening anyhow.'

'It's very interesting,' said Bognor, 'but I don't think

it's quite relevant to finding the murderer. All you're saying is that your father would have preferred Derby out of the way but that he didn't actually get him out of the way himself. So you've given me a new suspect and then taken him away again all in the same sentence.'

'That's not all,' said Harris. 'You see I think just possibly there's a tendency for everyone to go barking up the wrong tree. I mean I get the impression that because he was killed in our office and because he'd become an apparrently rather lonely old man in later days then everyone assumes that the murderer must be one of us. I don't think that's necessarily true. It's not even particularly likely.'

'I've heard that once before today,' said Bognor. 'In fact I get a distinct idea that you're all a bit worried.'

'Ha,' said Harris, 'remember Hanratty. What about Timothy Evans? If we had a little more confidence in the ability of the police to get the right man then perhaps we wouldn't be worried. As it is you're absolutely right, we're all terrified.'

Bognor yawned. It had been an exhausting day and it was nothing like over. The bottle of Krug was only half empty.

'There's no need to be terrified in this case,' he said. 'Sanders strikes me as being very able and sensible and dspite any appearance to the contrary I've never yet got the wrong person in any of the cases I've been involved in.'

'All right,' said Harris, 'then here are some ideas I think are worth pursuing. Have you for instance been to St John's flat?'

'No.'

'Well I think you should. The furniture is very fine—eighteenth century a lot of it, though he indulged a taste for Chinoiserie I don't share. The Chestertons which everyone joked about are all first editions and he also has several bits of correspondence. The Munnings and the Stubbs and the Augustus John are all originals and they weren't presents. Even the colour television and the record player suggest an affluence which isn't exactly consistent with the salary we paid him.'

'Which was?'

'Under five.'

Bognor raised his eyebrows. 'What about the expenses? I thought all journalists lived on their expenses.'

'Not on the *Globe* they don't. It's my father's religious background of which you're no doubt aware. And the perks of that job aren't all they're cracked up to be either—the odd free meal, the odd free drink, the odd trip. But St John spent every holiday in Florence or Venice and he always stayed at the Villa Medici or the Gritti Palace. His favourite drinks were Lafite, Latour and Jack Daniels. Do you see what I'm getting at?'

'He must have had private means of some kind.'

Bertie shrugged. 'It's hardly likely,' he said. 'His father was a butcher in Leeds. Rather an unsuccessful butcher too, I believe.'

'So how did he do it?'

'That's what I'm asking you. He hardly won it at bridge. All I'm suggesting is that he managed to convey the impression of living on an income of at the very least ten grand a year. Which is about three times what we know he earned. If you could find out how he filled the gap then I suggest further that you might be nearer a solution. I say no more. I honestly don't know any more except that there was something distinctly rat-like about Derby. Now drink up your Krug and let's put the world to rights in the Samuel Pepys office.'

4

When they returned Lord Wharfedale's paragraph had arrived.

'St John Derby,' it read, 'who died yesterday was

that rare character, a legend in his own time. In recent years he had edited this column with unequalled flair and panache but before that his oils were spread over a wider canvas. The obituary which appears on page 12 gives some indication of a career which took him from Carlisle to the Caucasus, from West Ham to West Africa and in which he conversed with the great names of our century from Hitler to Marilyn Monroe.

'Nevertheless we who work for this column, while joining in the public tribute to one of the great professionals of Fleet Street, also remember him as a man.

'Always ready with an apt quip, never wounding, always gay, he was generous to a fault, particularly where younger less experienced colleagues were concerned.

'A favourite story he often told was how as a young war correspondent in Abyssinia he found himself battling for a scoop with Colonel Erskine Prothero, doyen of foreign correspondents and then at the peak of his powers as "The Man in the News".

' "Young man," said Prothero, "be happy while y'er leevin', for y'er a lang time deid." '

'It was an adage of which St John Derby never lost sight. He will be much missed.'

'Would you re-type this please, Simon?' said Mr Gringe.

'And cut out the adjectives?' he said facetiously, but Mr Gringe did not smile.

'We are not supposed to take more than two hours for lunch even if covering a function. It is now four fifteen and I must have your copy by six at the latest.'

Bognor tried to look contrite and went to his desk. Luckily this was in a corner and he was able to conceal some of his confusion, ineptitude and simple drunkenness by turning his back to the room and talking very softly into the telephone when required to do so. There were no incoming calls but he managed to contact the man from Cheltenham and the press officer of the Regiment. By ten to six he had completed his paragraphs and handed them to Gringe. Five minutes later as he idled through the *Evening Standard* he was aware of a presence at his elbow.

'Room for improvement, Mr Bognor, but in the circumstances not a bad try. What did Queen Charlotte's say about the Countess of Cornwall?'

'They didn't. They said they couldn't comment.'

In fact Bognor had been too embarrassed to ring the hospital. He rather hoped to palm the story off on Molly Mortimer next morning.

'Ah,' said Mr Gringe, 'better try the Countess herself tomorrow. I like the way you handled the Prince of Wales Midland Light Infantry.'

'I only cut out a couple of adjectives. Otherwise I just typed it straight out. Their chap didn't have anything to add.'

'That's not the point. It reads very well. It's just as important to know when to leave well alone, don't you think?' Mr Gringe seemed to invest this last remark with gigantic significance. Bognor wondered why. 'However there are one or two points. This headline you've put on the joke outside the church. I don't quite understand it.'

Bognor had captioned the story 'Vicarious fun' and was rather pleased with it. 'It's a pun,' he said, 'on vicar.'

'I'm not an idiot. I can see it's a pun on vicar, but why vicarious? There's nothing vicarious about it. Vicarious means substitutive. A form of delegation. Vicarious fun is fun which doesn't fully involve you. It doesn't apply here.'

'You're quite right. It seemed a good idea at the time. What else was wrong?'

'Nothing very vital. It's just a question of tightening up generally, employing less discursiveness, getting to the point sooner. I think,' again he seemed exaggeratedly portentous, 'it would be a help if you were to come to the point more quickly.'

'How do you mean?' Bognor still couldn't be certain if he was saying more than one thing at a time. 'In my stories, or generally?'

'Of course,' said Mr Gringe, tight lipped, and even more Delphically. Then he smiled. 'Never mind,' he said. 'I think that all in all we've made quite a promising start, although I must ask you to try to stick to reasonable office hours. It is a hazard of this sort of job to be, er waylaid, by all sorts of temptations. Please try to resist it. Now I don't think you've met Horace Peckwater.'

Horace Peckwater was the man who trimmed the stories into shape and prepared them for the printers, the man who stayed until late in the evening supervising the translation of the messy typewriting into clean legible print suitable for several million pairs of eyes. Mr Peckwater was laconic to a degree. In response to Bognor's attempts to introduce and then ingratiate himself he replied with three words used at wide intervals: ' 'Evening,' 'Yes,' and 'No.' Bognor decided to inquire about Mr Peckwater, but decided also that any enquiries would be better directed to a third party.

At six-thirty Mr Gringe pronounced the column complete and ready to go. The staff were therefore dismissed.

'Simon,' said Molly Mortimer, as they put on their coats, 'I'm looking in on this private view at the Western Fine Arts. Why don't you come?'

'I'd like to but I'm expected home. Sorry.'

'Oh dar*ling*. You'll never make a journalist. I'm sure she can wait. It won't take long.'

For a moment Bognor wrestled with conflicting thoughts. Any more to drink could well prove fatal and there would certainly be drink at a private view. The best thing for him would be a hot bath and an early night. On the other hand Molly Mortimer was definitely fanciable. And stimulating company. Above all he had a job to work on and solve within a week.

'Well,' he said. 'Provided it doesn't take too long. OK. Just let me make one phone call.'

He dialled the flat.

'Monica?'

'Yes.'

'I'm afraid I may be a bit late. Something's cropped up.'

'Have you been drinking?'

'No.'

'You bloody have.'

'Well. A bit. I mean a glass or two. You have to on this job.'

'You sound paralytic. The sooner you're home the safer you'll be.'

'Don't want to be safe.'

'Don't be silly. Where are you going?'

'An art gallery.'

'Oh. Parkinson rang.'

'What did he want? Why didn't he ring here?'

'He said he didn't want to "blow your cover". He seemed to think it was rather a joke actually. He laughed.'

'Doesn't sound like Parkinson. But what did he want?'

'He said to ring him in the morning. And that he'd found they had a file on someone called Milborn Port.'

'Really?'

'Yes. Is he real?'

'Only just. OK. I must rush. See you soon. Take care. 'Bye.'

The art gallery was like the Northern Line Tube train in the rush hour, only better dressed. Most of the women were in little black dresses although the elderly wore big black dresses with a variety of animals draped round their shoulders. The men were in dark suits of a quite different cut and cloth to those on view at the Dorchester earlier. These were waisted and double vented with, here and there, a hint of velvet or braiding. Pocket handkerchiefs protruded from almost every breast pocket. Brut after shave ladelled on by the spoonful mingled with marginally more feminine Chanel and Balenciaga. Here and there a champagne navvy in faded denim, casually knotted scarf and per-

haps a single gold earring lent a spurious Bohemianism
to the gathering.

Bognor signed the visitors' book, took a glass of
champagne from the man in the white jacket and
barged through to a small oasis of empty parquet floor,
closely followed by Molly.

'Phew,' he said, wiping sweat from his forehead and
smiling vacuously at a vicious fox, teeth bared, which
dangled from a scrawny neck just in front of him. 'Are
they always like this?'

'Always,' said Molly. 'This is emptier than most.'

'How on earth are you supposed to view the pictures?' Bognor noticed that nobody was even facing the
pictures, let alone trying to examine them.

'Silly. Private views are for viewing people not pictures. In any case most of these were in the colour mag
on Sunday.'

'Who are they by?'

'Sanguinetti.'

Bognor had a vague recollection of some incompre-
hensibly abstract objects hindered by a dense explana-
tory text.

'Theme on a bicycle chain?' he said, groping.

'That's right. Very successful.'

'To difficult for me,' said Bognor. 'I like my art traditional. Turner's about as way out as I can get.'

'I like my men traditional,' said Molly, flashing her
teeth. 'Oh look there's Dmitri. Let's go and talk to
him.'

'Dmitri who?'

'Dmitri Pugh. He does Parson Woodforde on the
Sunday News.'

'Oh God no. I sat next to Parson Woodforde at
lunch. He's unspeakable.'

'Nonsense,' said Molly briskly. 'He's divine.'

By this time they had pushed through to Dmitri who
Bognor realized to his great relief was not the Parson
Woodforde with whom he had shared lunch.

'Dmitri, darling,' exclaimed Molly, allowing herself
to be kissed noisily on the cheek. 'You've met Simon

Bognor. He sat next to you at lunch. He says you're unspeakable.'

'You had lunch at the Dorchester?' said Dmitri, who was small, elegant and sported a natty grey rinse and a Guards tie. 'That would have been Perkins, my leg man. I second your judgment. He *is* unspeakable but so are those food manufacturers. I should imagine you had an unspeakable lunch. I trust you didn't go on to the Liberace party afterwards.'

'No.'

'Just as well. Perkins returned from it at five-thirty unspeakable as usual and speechless too. Champagne cocktails at tea time, my dear, too too vulgar.' He turned to Molly. 'I was sad about St John. In fact *désolé*. I saw him at the Harbingers last night. Extraordinary, here today gone tomorrow. I shall write a note for Sunday of course.'

'Did you speak to him?' asked Molly.

'As a matter of fact I did. We had a natter before dinner and then afterwards I suggested we went on to Sally's but he said he had to meet someone. He seemed a bit out of sorts, I thought, but I put it down to the usual.'

'Did you say meet someone?' asked Bognor, but his question was drowned by the stentorian bellow of 'Ladies and Gentlemen, pray silence for . . .' Bognor recognized the voice of the toastmaster who had officiated at lunch and standing on tiptoes confirmed that it was indeed the same man, in the same ill-fitting jacket.

Dmitri and Molly swore in unison.

'I wouldn't have come if I'd known,' said Molly in a stage whisper. 'They *never* have speeches at the Western Fine Arts.'

'Waste of time anyway,' said Dimitri. ''Sanguinetti doesn't speak a word of English.'

Nevertheless there were speeches. First from the owner of the gallery, then from the diminutive and diffident Sanguinetti who had to have every word translated, inadequately, by a pretty Italian girl with enormous cow-like eyes, and finally a vote of thanks

and appreciation from a long-winded pseud who
claimed, according to Dmitri and Molly, to be London's leading art critic. During them Dmitri managed
to filch a full bottle from the waiter's tray. By the time
the art critic had finished speaking the combination of
boredom and drink had reduced Bognor to near insen-
sibility.

'Did you say meet someone?' he asked again.

'Sorry, dear boy,' said Dmitri. 'What?'

'Meet someone? St John Derby. Did he say he was
going to meet someone?'

'Yes,' said Dmitri. 'Sorry, excuse me but I must have
a word with Sanguinetti about bicycle chains.' He
kissed Molly goodbye and disappeared in the crowd.
Bognor suddenly felt very weak.

'I'm awfully sorry,' he said, 'but I really think I'd
better get home. I seem to have been drinking all day
and I'm not used to it.'

Molly looked at him, and smiled sympathetically.
'Darling,' she said, 'you've gone quite white. I really
don't think I would trust you to get home. Come on.'

She took hold of Bognor by the elbow and propelled
him towards the door, smiling and exchanging the odd
word with fellow guests as she went. Outside, by good
fortune, a taxi was just depositing a late arrival. Molly
opened the door, pushed Bognor in, gave an address to
the driver, and climbed in after him. Bognor shut his
eyes and burped noisily.

'That's better,' he said. 'I'm afraid I've had a skin-
ful.'

'Just go to sleep,' said Molly. 'It will take a quarter
of an hour to get there.'

'Where?'

'Go to sleep.'

Bognor shrugged, nodded, burped again and closed
his eyes. He hadn't felt so grim for ages. Thank God
he only had a week of Fleet Street to do. Otherwise he
certainly wouldn't last the pace. He prayed he wouldn't
be sick in the taxi. After a moment he dozed off. He
woke briefly five minutes later and saw that they were

driving along a tunnel. It must be the Hyde Park underpass.

'This isn't the way home.'

'Not your way home may be, but my way home.'

'Am I going home with you?'

'Yes.'

'How very improper.'

'The only improper thing is your present condition. You're paralytic.'

'That's the second time someone said that this evening.'

'It's true.'

'Don't tell, will you.'

Molly laughed softly. 'Why should I tell?' she asked. 'And who?'

But Bognor had dozed off again.

He didn't really come round until he was in her flat. He was sitting on one of those PVC sacks filled with polystyrene. Dimly he realized that he was unlikely to be able to get up without help. He tried to focus on the wall opposite which was covered in hessian and lithographs. There was a leopardskin rug on the floor and a huge fireplace with row upon row of printed invitations on the mantelpiece.

'Feeling any better?' Molly came in carrying a tray with a steaming half pint mug and a bottle of Alka Seltzer. 'Drink this,' she said, 'I've made it black.' She'd changed into a long, low cut house-dress which clung to her hips. To Bognor she looked infinitely desirable.

'And there's no point in looking at me like that,' she said. 'You're far too drunk.'

'Like what?'

'Like that. Underneath your bland, chubby exterior Simon Bognor I suspect there lurks the Blagdon amateur rapist.'

'The what?'

'Surely you read *Private Eye*?'

'Oh yes. I see what you mean. Ouch.' The coffee was boiling and he'd burnt the roof of his mouth.

'Drink it all,' she said, 'and take two Alka Seltzer.'

'Oh, God,' he said, sipping nervously, 'what's the time? Monica will be going spare.'

'In fact it's only just after eight,' she said. 'You got your drinking done early. So Monica won't be going spare just yet. She won't go spare till she sees you.'

Slowly he finished the mug. Molly came back with another and when he was halfway through it she said, 'Feeling anything approaching sober?'

'I'm not as drunk as all that.'

'Simon darling, you are quite as drunk as all that. More so.'

'Well I'm sobering now. I'm quite sober.' It was true that the coffee and the Alka Seltzer were removing the cotton wool feeling. He still felt sick.

'I'm a bit queasy,' he said, 'but quite sober.'

'All right,' she said. 'I'll try to go slowly. Stop me if you don't understand.'

'OK'

'Right.' She took a cigarette from the mantelpiece and lit it, breathing out smoke slowly. It reminded Bognor of Bertie Harris. Suddenly he felt a lot more sober.

'Granny Gringe says you once worked for a paper called the *Eagle* in Winnipeg,' said Molly, slowly as she'd promised.

'That's right,' said Simon, adrenalin starting to flow. 'What about it?'

'No such thing,' she said softly, shaking her head and looking at Simon with amusement coupled with kind contempt.

'Don't be ridiculous,' he said, feebly. 'I ought to know. I worked for it.'

'You're the one who's being ridiculous. First of all I looked it up in the reference books and it wasn't there. So then I rang the press attaché at the Canadian High Commission and he confirmed it.'

'It must have gone bust.'

'Simon, will you stop being pig-headed. I am trying to make things easier for you and I'm going to try to help you. There is not and there never has been a paper called the *Winnipeg Eagle*. You claimed that you had worked for a paper called by that name and therefore you were telling a lie. The only possible reason for telling us a lie like that would be to persuade us that you are a real life journalist which you obviously are not.'

'How do you know?'

'Can't take your drink for a start. Also you have an untapped vein of innocence running deep down inside which most journalists have mined by the time they're twenty-five. So if you're not a journalist what are you?'

'You're being silly.'

Molly puffed impatiently. 'You arrive in the office on the very day that the boss of the column is murdered. Nobody mentioned you were coming the day before. It was a total surprise to all of us. You were sent on the personal orders of Lord Wharfedale which is unusual. In other words if it wasn't for your unconventional appearance it would be quote obvious to all and sundry that you're some sort of plain clothes policeman.'

'What if I am?'

'If you are I'd like to help.'

'Oh all right. It strikes me that everyone on the bloody Pepys column is a lot more keen on detection than I am.'

He handed her the identity card, and she read it, eyebrows raised in amused half-belief.

'Board of Trade,' she said, appraising him for a moment, 'I'd have said Treasury myself. However it's better than the Post Office or the Ministry of Agriculture.'

'We do cover areas which are not strictly speaking the province of the Board.'

'Clearly.'

'You said you could help.'

'Yes.'

'Well?'

'You know I once had a brief fling with old St John?'

'You denied it this morning. Not very convincingly.'

'That was because of the appalling Milborn. He's the

one man on the column I have never laid a finger on.
He resents it.' She crossed her legs and Bognor again
felt sexual stirrings deep down inside him.

'So what?' he said.

'Nothing except that I'm afraid I threw him over for
Bertie. That's a bit dramatic. Anything between me
and Bertie's always been entirely superficial and I
thought the same applied to St John. Then he came
round to my flat and made a scene. He got rather
over-excited about it all and mucked it up by bringing
me plastic roses—very good ones—to symbolize the
everlasting nature of his undying love.'

'That was rather sweet.'

'Except that when I rejected him he threw them on
the fire. The smell . . . God it was dreadful.'

You bitch, thought Bognor wanting her even more.
She laughed.

'I don't see where this gets us,' he said.

'Ever since then he became a real pain. He'd cut
back my expenses, call me in on my Sunday off, stop
me going on foreign trips, that sort of thing. Then I
had an affair with Arlington Fingest.'

Bognor grinned. Arlo Fingest was now Minister for
Overseas Development. A Catholic; his young, beauti-
ful and numerous progeny and his immaculate and
handsome novelist wife were much advertised in the
press. He presented a public picture of utter fidelity,
yet even Bognor had heard rumours.

'The Member for Barnes?'

'Yes. He's a poppet but a two-timing, hypocritical
poppet. And very good . . . never mind. St John found
out.'

'How?'

'He found a letter in my drawer. He intercepted a
phone call. He saw us in a restaurant.'

'All by chance?'

Molly arched her eyebrows. 'Are you feeling better?'
she asked. Bognor nodded. 'Do you think you'll
remember this in the morning?'

He grimaced. 'I don't know.'

'If you were a journalist you'd write it down. That's why journalists are supposed to do shorthand. They're too drunk to trust their memory. Usually too hung over to read their notes the next day but that's another story.'

'Aren't you exaggerating?'

'Of course I'm exaggerating, darling. That's journalism too.'

Bognor suppressed another burp. 'Anyway,' he said, 'St John Derby found out you were having an affair with Arlington Fingest. Then what?'

'He tried to blackmail us.'

'Us?'

'Him.'

'Are you sure?'

'Of course I'm sure.' She got up and went over to a trolley loaded with bottles from which she helped herself to a Scotch. For a second she looked at Bognor inquiringly and then said, 'That coffee's having a remarkable effect but I don't think you're ready for a drink, do you?' He winced back at her and wondered if she had to wear a corset. She was remarkably flat tummied.

'I don't have any letters if that's what you mean,' she went on. 'St John was far too sly to put it in writing. He asked Arlo round to his club for dinner, said he wanted to pick his brains about some stories and then tried to blackmail him over the brandy. Arlo stalled and came to me. I fixed it.'

'How?'

'Child's-play. I told St John I didn't give a bugger who knew that I was having it off with Arlington Fingest and that I for my part would rather see him in the nick for blackmail than pay up, even if it did mean the end of a promising career and a lovely relationship.'

'What happened then?'

'St John stayed out of the nick, the promising career flourished and the lovely relationship came to an end.'

'Why?'

'St John believed me, which was just as well because I wasn't bluffing.'

'It can't have helped your relationship with him.'

'On the contrary. He bought me lunch at the Connaught and we became the best of friends again. It appealed to his sense of humour.'

'And Fingest?'

'Fingest was thoroughly ungrateful and rather huffy. He thought I'd trifled with his career and trifled with his affections, and since to be honest the only things I had actually trifled with were his body and his cheque book I was glad to be rid of him. I never went near his affections let alone his career.'

Bognor sighed. The adrenalin was on the wane and he was feeling sleepy again. 'I'm fascinated,' he said, 'and it's kind of you to be so frank, but I don't see why this is relevant. I mean it's years ago. You're surely not suggesting that St John Derby was murdered by the Minister of Overseas Development because of an extra-marital indiscretion committed in Opposition.'

'Opposition? Opposition to what?' It was Molly's turn to be bemused.

'To the Government. He was only an opposition MP when it happened.'

'I have had ministers,' she pouted, self deprecatingly. 'Not very senior ministers I admit, but still ministers.'

Bognor felt mounting frustration, sexual and conversational.

'Where does this get us?' he asked.

'Sorry,' she said, 'I forgot you'd had so much to drink. St John Derby tried to blackmail my lover about ten years ago. He didn't succeed because of me but nevertheless he handled it with quite a high degree of sophistication. If Fingest had been involved with some professional tart or a married woman who had more to lose than me, then he'd have coughed up.'

'How much did St John ask?'

'I don't remember. Quite a modest sum, but he'd have been back for more. They always are. The point is it all came quite naturally to him. Second nature, you could say.'

'You mean he blackmailed other people?'

'I don't know for certain but it seems very likely. I can't believe Fingest was the only one.'

'No. Do you *know* if he blackmailed anyone else? Anyone on the column for instance?'

'I doubt it. Everyone always assumes that gossip columnists sleep around, and drink and take drugs, so there's no opportunity to blackmail them. But he must have been getting money from somewhere and you can be sure it wasn't bloody Wharfedale Newspapers. Rich as Croesus and mean as Scrooge. You learn a lot about the foibles of the rich and famous doing our sort of job. It's an obvious base for a professional blackmailer.'

Bognor frowned and tried to concentrate.

'I'm going to give you one small drink to help you think,' said Molly, 'and then home to bed.'

'I don't want another drink,' said Bognor feebly, but she poured out a cognac and another Scotch for herself.

'So,' he said, 'all I have to do is find out who he was getting money from and eliminate from there.' He sipped. 'You're the second person today who's pointed out the disparity between Derby's money and his earned income.'

'And who was the first?'

'Bertie Harris, actually.'

'Bertie would know the exact salary, and he's not exactly unobservant. I could tell you a thing or two about him.'

'Do.'

'Some other time.' She looked at her watch. 'It's getting late. You'd better get to your girl before she really does go spare.'

Bognor made a face. He had forgotten about Monica and he was getting drunk again. She was going to be censorious and unsympathetic. Getting to his feet was going to be the problem, he decided. These sacks were very relaxing but it wasn't easy to extricate yourself at the best of times and this certainly wasn't that. At the second attempt he managed it.

'Oh dear Simon,' she said, stubbing out a cigarette, her fifth at least. 'You *are* in trouble. That cognac wasn't wise.'

'I know,' he said. 'I told you so.'

'No willpower, Mr Bognor,' she said, laughing. 'Come on, I'll help you out.' She armed him to the lift, which was tiny. So small that they had to stand very close. Bognor felt more sexual stirrings.

'Who,' he asked, 'do you think might have a clue about Derby's blackmailees?'

'I'd start with Anthea Morrison,' said Molly, as the lift clanged to the ground floor, 'she doesn't miss anything that girl, though I don't think anyone else realizes how much she takes in. They're all wildly indiscreet with her. And occasionally she has provided a shoulder to cry on. She kept St John's diary too.'

They were out in the street now and she pulled her arms round her chest and shivered. A light sleet was falling and the pavement was slippery with slush. 'Sloane Square's just down there,' she said, pointing left where the street turned a corner fifty yards away. 'It's not far and there's a taxi rank. I'd come with you only it's too bloody cold and I'm not wearing anything.' She stamped her feet. 'Are you going to be all right? She put her hands out and placed them on his cheeks, staring at him for a second. 'You look terrible,' she said softly. 'Absolutely bloody terrible. But I think you'll make it.' She leant forward and kissed him lightly on the lips. 'See you tomorrow,' she said, and turned back through the swing doors into the block.

Bognor set off uncertainly. The street was deserted and ill lit and he was smashed out of his mind. The last cognac had set the alcohol in motion again and he could scarcely see where he was going. He set his sights on a lamp-post at the junction of the street and a small alley, and steered towards it.

'A kiss,' he muttered to himself. 'A small kiss but a kiss nonetheless.' Light as a gossamer's wing. More of a peck than a kiss, but it had been on the lips. It could have been on a cheek. That would have been different.

No hint of promise in a kiss on the cheek however sensuous, but a kiss on the lips, even one as light as a gossamer's wing. What was a gossamer's wing anyway? Had he got it right? It didn't much matter. Did she fancy him? Did she fancy everyone? Not Milborn Port. Was he in love? Maybe not but she had kissed him. On the lips.

The lamp-post, he realized suddenly, was not getting any closer. He must have stopped. He retched slightly and began to place one foot in front of the other counting the steps as he went. At twenty the lamp-post was almost in touching distance and he was just debating whether or not to make a lunge for it when a figure emerged from the alley. The face was hidden under a wide brimmed hat but there was no mistaking the menace in the heavily hunched shoulders.

You pig,' said the figure. 'Just piss off and stay clear, and let this be a warning.' And as he uttered these peculiar words he swung his fist in a great arc. Bognor watched fascinated and quite unable to move as the fist advanced towards him, gathering pace inexorably, before it landed firmly in the middle of his face. As it did so he felt another blow on the back of his head, and then everything stopped and he had a dim distant sensation of falling that he associated vaguely with being given gas at the dentist's. 'Help', he tried to say. 'Stop,' he tried to say. But through the blackness and the pain he was aware that he was producing no more coherent sound than an obscene gurgle.

'My God,' said Monica. 'My God.'

'It's all right, miss,' said the taxi-driver. 'He's not as bad as he looks. Least ways if he is it's the booze more than the blood. Is he yours then?'

Bognor who was unable to remain upright without leaning heavily on the public-spirited driver tried to say something, but it hurt too much. Besides he could think of nothing sensible to say. Another gurgle emerged from his mouth accompanied by a dribble of blood.

'It's one pound fifty,' said the driver. 'If he's yours that is.'

'Yes,' said Monica, eyes starting from her head, 'I'm afraid he is mine. Could you bring him in and put him somewhere . . . somewhere safe. Oh my God.'

The taxi-driver helped Bognor into the flat and put him almost gently into an armchair before accepting two pounds from Monica.

'He just turned up at the rank in Sloane Square,' he said, in response to her question, 'staggering around something terrible and spitting blood all over the auction. Couple of other blokes wouldn't take him 'cos he'd make a mess of their cabs but I'd got some old newspapers so I put him on those. It's not as bad as it looks like I say. Nothing broke. Still got all his teeth. It's his liver I'm worried about.'

'You've been very kind,' said Monica, taking another pound from her purse. 'I don't know what he'd have done without you.'

'Got home in the morning,' said the driver, pocketing the extra pound. 'Don't you worry, miss. He'll be OK tomorrow. Bruise and a headache that's all he'll have.' He let himself out and Monica turned back to the bloody Bognor.

'What ever happened?' she asked.

Through the messy pain of blood and brandy and champagne Bognor thought she looked rather plain. She had already taken off her make-up ready for bed and was wearing an old quilted dressing gown and felt bedroom slippers. For a moment he toyed with the idea of telling her she didn't look so hot herself, then thought better of it. Instead, with an effort he pointed at his nose and mimed a right hook.

'Surely you can say *something*,' said Monica. 'Oh I wish you did something sensible for a living. I wish you worked in an office.'

'I've been in a bloody office,' shouted Bognor, and then let out another grunt of pain. It had been a very hurtful sentence.

'It's no use,' said Monica, 'I can't understand. And

you stink of alcohol. I'll fetch some cotton wool. Try to get undressed.'

When she came back with a bowl full of boiling water and cotton wool swabs Bognor had managed to take off his overcoat and his tie. She looked at him crossly for a second and then smiled. 'Oh, Simon,' she said, her eyes misting with tears, 'I do wish you'd look after yourself.' Bognor nodded. 'Would you like a brandy or something?' Bognor retched and then shook his head.

'You sounded as if you were plastered when I rang earlier,' she said, kneeling down and starting to dab at the blood which had clotted round his nose and mouth. 'But I didn't imagine you'd come back like this. I think I'd better use some witch hazel.'

Bognor shook his head violently. It would sting.

'Darling,' she said, 'there's nothing else. I haven't any steak.'

He shrugged and she went on dabbing.

'Open wide.' He opened wide and she smiled.

'The taxi-driver was right,' she said, kissing him lightly on the nose.

It reminded Bognor of the kiss from Molly earlier on. He remembered it nostalgically then checked himself. Hell, he thought, they're just two completely different sorts of woman.

'All teeth present and correct,' said Monica. 'Now listen. I know you can't talk but while I'm cleaning you up I'm afraid I've got bad news. You're not the only person who's been in the wars. Only I'm afraid,' she stopped for a second, 'I'm afraid the other person wasn't quite so lucky. Parkinson rang half an hour ago.'

'Ow!' Bognor yelped. She had pressed too hard just below his nose, which he judged from the way he was feeling was the point of maximum impact. He was suddenly filled with a sense of impending disaster.

'Pencil and paper,' he managed to say, every syllable excruciating. Monica looked disapproving but brought it nonetheless.

'Not Anthea Morrison?' he wrote in block capitals. Monica looked at him in astonishment. 'How on earth did you know?'

He shrugged. He hadn't known. It was that flicker of premonition. Molly Mortimer had been the second person that day to suggest that the Pepys secretary might be able to help him more than anyone else, and yet she was, apart from the monosyllabic Peckwater, the only member of the column's staff he hadn't had any words with at all. Not about murders anyway. Only about amateur theatrical companies in Gloucestershire and regiments marching about with their bayonets fixed and where the paper clips were kept and whether he preferred Indian or China tea in the afternoons. He swore and winced.

'She fell under a tube train at Blackfriars,' said Monica, 'during the rush hour. No one seems quite sure how it happened. Apparently it was terribly crowded. There are so few trains at the moment with the go-slow. She was right at the front of the platform and the crowd had piled up behind her and she fell off just as the train was coming into the station.'

'Fell?' wrote Bognor.

'In the circumstances,' said Monica straightening up, and looking distastefully at the stained swabs and the muddy water, 'I should say she was pushed. Parkinson didn't offer an opinion. All he said was that you were on secondment and that if it wasn't for civil servants having to obey politicians who are prepared to toady to newspaper proprietors you wouldn't be in this mess. Instead he said, if I remember rightly, that you should be tucked up safely in the basement at the Board of Trade with your code book.'

She took the bowl away and came back with his pyjamas, the Viyella ones with the frayed cord. 'I agree with Parkinson,' she said, 'but since you are in this mess we'd better get you tucked up in bed here.' She unbuttoned him, untied him, unzipped him, allowed him the faint dignity of removing his own underpants and made him a mug of hot chocolate. He was sitting up in bed drinking it when he remembered something else. He mouthed for pen and paper.

'No. You've done yourself enough damage for one day.'

He shaped his hands into a gesture of prayer and tried to blow her a kiss. It hurt too much and he gave up but she smiled and relented.

'One final message,' she said. 'And then you will finish your cocoa and I will turn out the light.'

He took the pad and tried to remember. It was too much effort. He signed to her to bring him his jacket and he felt in the pocket for a little before extricating a crumpled scrap from a notebook.

In the city set upon slime and loam
They cry in their parliament 'Who goes home?'

He read it through and then penciled in three dots and a question mark after the last word before handing it to Monica. She looked at it briefly.

'Chesterton,' she said after a few seconds of brow furrowing. '*The Flying Inn*, I think. Do you want me to check?'

He nodded and she went out. Bognor found himself warming to her once again. She had her faults and she wasn't all that much to look at but she was reliable. A good person to have at one's back, when the chips were down and all that. Nothing flash. But sound. A good egg.

She returned holding open a faded scarlet volume entitled *A G. K. Chesterton Omnibus*.

'I was right,' she said, '*The Flying Inn* it is. Do you want me to read it?'

Bognor nodded.

'First four lines only,' she said, 'then lights out.'

In the city set upon slime and loam
They cry in their parliament 'Who goes home?'
And there comes no answer in arch or dome
For none in the city of graves goes home.

She made a face. 'Rather horrid,' she said. 'I prefer it when he's being rude about Grocers or funny about rolling English roads. Now before you pass out I am going to make you sleep.' She confiscated his chocolate and turned the lights out but it was more than an hour before Bognor slept. Despite the pain and the knockout punch he couldn't sleep. Instead he kept repeating in a lilting whisper:

> And there comes no answer in arch or dome
> For none in the city of graves goes home.

He was too fuddled to know what it could mean but the general tone was evident enough. Even if it was only an idle doodle St John Derby's thoughts had been singularly gloomy on the night of his death. 'For none in the city of graves goes home.' Had he been waiting for someone? For someone he feared might kill him. He tried to remember what that tiny man with the improbable name had said, Dmitri Pugh, that was it. 'He said he had to meet someone . . . he seemed out of sorts.' So Derby had been sitting in his office drunk and out of sorts and waiting for someone, and while he was waiting he wrote about graves and people not going home. But he'd ordered a taxi. Perhaps his nerve had failed him. Or maybe he was being optimistic.

'For none in the city of graves goes home.' Bognor shuddered.

5

To say that he felt better next morning was accurate, but to say that he felt well hyperbole. His head ached with hangover and his face ached from the stranger's punch. At the back of his head there was another area of intense discomfort where he must have hit the lamp-post on the way down to the pavement. His stomach was like jelly and his hands shook. Speech now seemed to hurt him less but his lips were so swollen that he sounded like an apprentice ventriloquist. The first time he stood to go to the lavatory he had to sit down abruptly to stop the room revolving. Nevertheless he was still short of breath and as the moments of waking ticked by and he sipped at strong black tea and ate toast and home made marmalade he began to feel that conceivably the day could be faced. Not, he decided, with optimism. Not even with equanimity. But faced all the same.

Five minutes later he was not so sure. First he saw that Anthea Morrison's death was on the front page of his second paper, the *Daily Express*. Some bright executive there had noticed the connection. 'Secretary in death fall' was the headline and the story which followed was a perfectly straightforward account of the tragedy even if it was written in odd English. The final paragraph was the real reason for the story being so prominently displayed. 'Miss Morrison's death,' it ran, 'came less than twenty-four hours after the sudden death of the distinguished journalist St John Derby (Obituary, page 9). Mr Derby was editor of the Samuel Pepys column of the *Daily Globe* where Miss Morrison worked as a secretary.'

Bognor had just finished reading it when the phone rang. It was, inevitably, Parkinson. After several futile attempts to explain to Parkinson first that he *had* got the right number, secondly that he *was* Simon Bognor and thirdly that he was *not* drunk, he handed the phone to Monica, who did her best to explain for him.

'He'd like you to drop in on your way to work,' she said, when she'd done so. 'He wasn't sympathetic about your wounds.'

Bognor grunted. It was bad enough trying to eat toast with your mouth fixed in a permanent grin. Parkinson and the *Daily Express* were making life worse.

As he dressed he fastened paper to a clip board and began to make the notes to which he always resorted in times of crisis. In this case it was almost as important to put the garbled events of the previous day into some order as it was to establish motives and methods and opportunities for murder. 'Interviews,' he wrote, 'with Wharfedale, Gringe, Mortimer, Port, Wimbledon, Harris and Mortimer again.' He rubbed his lip and thought of gossamer wings. 'And Father of Chapel and Imperial Father,' he added by way of afterthought. Then he wrote underneath: 'Unresolved—two murders, one assault . . .' He chewed at the pencil. There were plenty of other unresolved questions. Had Lord Wharfedale really been trying to sack Derby and had he been prevented from doing so by the Union? It seemed improbable. 'Ask Imperial Father,' he wrote. Then there was St John Derby's unexplained wealth and the suggestion of blackmail. Molly Mortimer had come right out with it. Bertie Harris's insinuation had been oblique but it was obvious that he was implying blackmail. That said something about their respective characters. And Parkinson had mentioned something about a file on Milborn Port. A file on Milborn Port? Oh really. He kissed Monica on the cheek.

'Thank you for the city of graves,' he said, 'and everything.'

She smiled. 'Please be more careful today,' she said. 'Don't drink so much, stay away from dark alleyways and keep a stiff upper lip.'

'I don't have any option,' he said with feeling. He walked to the bus stop, determined today to behave more like a staid Board of Trade investigator and less like a cub reporter. It was bitterly cold again. He thrust his hands deep in his overcoat pocket and tried unsuccessfully to whistle a happy tune.

Parkinson was sitting stiffly in his upright chair stirring tea in a thick china cup with a chip. He looked, as usual, grim, but the spectre of a smile crossed his face when he saw Bognor's battered visage.

'I have never,' he said, with malicious satisfaction, 'known a man who was able to get to the centre of a problem as quickly as you, Bognor. It could even be

said that within a matter of hours you invariably become the centre of the problem yourself. I do appreciate that you like to become involved in your job. I do
really. But a certain detachment. A certain detachment.' He was stirring his tea with such venom that a
spoonful slopped on to his blotter where it was slowly
absorbed leaving a light brown stain. 'It is not necessary or desirable to cast yourself in the role of victim,
Bognor,' he said.

Bognor stared unhappily at the portrait of the Queen
which he could see just behind Parkinson's left ear and
said nothing.

Parkinson consulted his notes. 'First,' he said, 'I
have had a personal call from the Minister. The Minister has changed his mind. It's his prerogative and one
which he exercises mercilessly. He wants you off this
case. He admits he made a mistake. Unfortunately it's
a bit late for that.'

'Oh?' For a moment Bognor had seen a glimmer of
hope. A suggestion that he could return to a safe boring life in the basement.

'For a start,' said Parkinson, 'you're too closely involved already. Not that by itself that would normally
worry me. I don't like bowing to the self-seeking whims
of careerist politicians and it's not my business to curry
favour with Lord Wharfedale even if it's the Minister's.
But there is the file on Milborn Port.'

'What does the file say?'

Again Parkinson consulted his papers. 'Age fifty-
three, married, two sons, educated Sherborne and Trinity College, Dublin. Moscow Correspondent of *Daily
Globe* 1958. Gossip writer.'

'Just because he was once in Moscow that doesn't
make him . . .'

Parkinson glowered at him. 'Are you really not able
to speak more distinctly than that?' he asked. 'I am
having the greatest difficulty in comprehending whatever it is that you have to say.'

'Sorry . . . sir.'

'It's not a very big file,' said Parkinson drily, 'because your friend Mr Port is not a very big fish. As even you can appreciate he would have problems of access to anything of strategic importance or economic importance. On the other hand he is peculiarly well placed to provide information of what you would doubtless describe as social significance.'

'I don't quite follow.'

Parkinson twitched with exasperation. 'Have you ever heard of a filth man?'

'No.'

'A filth man, as the name suggests, is someone who gets the dirt on people. The idea's American but nowadays we're all interested in a little filth. Who's sleeping with whom, who's losing a fortune at the gaming tables, who's so consistently drunk he is unable to do his job, whose daughter has freaked out, whose wife has left him. People pay money for that sort of information. They're interested in it. It can be useful.'

'And Milborn Port was passing on that sort of thing to the Russian Embassy.'

'I'm delighted you're able to follow me so swiftly. It's not in the legal sense treason. He doesn't, as far as I know, possess state secrets but he makes mischief and we'd like to know a little more about him.'

Bognor was intrigued. 'Would they pay much?'

'Enough.'

'Enough to buy Château Lafite and pay the rent of a flashy flat in South Kensington?'

'Your Mr Port has a house in Stoke Poges.'

'I know.'

For once it was Parkinson's turn to look puzzled. 'It wouldn't be a lot of money. Not under the circumstances. Perhaps a few hundred a year. Why?'

'I have a theory.'

Parkinson put a hand to his forehead. 'I'd rather you didn't,' he said.

'What do you want me to do then?'

'Carry on. Not as before. Keep a low profile. Liaise with the police but for Christ's sake steer clear of trouble. I'm not interested in your solving the case. I would like information. And don't let on that you know about Milborn Port. Apart from anything else I don't want any confusion with Special Branch. They can be jealous.'

Bognor left, deflated. At the *Globe* he made two stops before reaching the Pepys office. First he called on Bert Watson, the Imperial Father. He'd never heard any mention of Lord Wharfedale trying to sack St John Derby and he doubted whether the chapel would have opposed the move. He had a shrewd notion that Derby wasn't a member of the Union anyway. Bognor expressed no surprise and in answer to Mr Watson's sympathetic enquiries about his swollen features, said he'd fallen down stairs in the flat when the lights fused.

He was more honest with the policeman.

'Did you see his face?' asked Sanders when he'd finished.

'Too dark, I'm afraid, and he had a hat pulled down over his eyes.'

'Scarf?'

'I don't think so. Why?'

Sanders lit another of the Embassy cigarettes whose fumes had already severely reduced the visibility in his office. 'You saw the papers?' he said.

'About Anthea Morrison.'

'Yes. Was it an accident?'

Sanders shrugged. 'What do you think?'

'I think she was pushed.'

The policeman stood up, came round the desk and bent down to examine the bruising. 'Must hurt,' he said laconically, 'and he wasn't wearing a scarf?'

'As I said I don't think so, but why?'

'Anthea Morrison was killed at about ten to seven. It appears that work stopped on your column at about half past six and she went straight to Blackfriars underground station to catch a train home. Normally it would have been after the rush hour but because of the go-slow there were still a lot of commuters around. Some of them stop off for a couple of pints and hope everyone else will have vanished by the time they get to the station . . . anyway, she was standing at the far end of the west-bound platform which is badly lit and she was standing in the front next to the line and she fell under the Richmond train. Nobody honestly knows what really happened but several of the people waiting near her say that there was a man in a dark overcoat standing just behind her. He had a hat pulled over his eyes and a scarf over the lower part of his face, which was normal enough as it was so perishing cold. The second she'd fallen he was off like a startled rabbit, muttering something about fetching an ambulance.'

'And did he?'

'Someone did. Could have been him. It was too late for her. She was a very nasty mess but she wouldn't have known much about it.'

Bognor visualized that terrible moment of falling, the fraction of a second between the time she was pushed to the time she hit the electric rail. He wondered if she'd been killed by that or by the impact of the train. He decided he didn't want to ask. Whichever it had been there was still time for her to realize what was happening.

'And no one stopped him?'

Sanders shook his head. 'No reason to. There was complete pandemonium for the first couple of minutes, especially near where she'd been. Further up the platform it was different. Anyway he got right away, guilty or not.' He paused and lit a new cigarette with the stub of the old one. 'What time did you say you were attacked?'

'I'm not sure. About half past eight I should say. I can check.'

Sanders pursed his lips. 'Dark overcoat, hat pulled down, and no scarf.'

'I'm not sure about the scarf.'

'And Sloane Square can't take more than half an hour from Blackfriars by any form of transport. Even the underground in a work-to-rule.'

'You mean that the man who killed Anthea Morrison was the same person who bashed me?'

'I don't think it's stretching coincidence too far.'

Bognor thought, something his various pains made unpleasant. Nor were the thoughts very happy.

'It has to be someone on the column,' he said eventually.

'Why so?'

'Because only my colleagues on the column knew that I was going off with Molly Mortimer.'

'Or the private viewers at the Western Fine Arts?'

'But they couldn't have got to the gallery from Blackfriars in time.'

Sanders agreed. 'Could be a conspiracy,' he ventured. 'Miss Mortimer might have telephoned to say you were with her.'

'Hardly.'

Sanders looked almost as miserable as Bognor. 'There's something implausibly whimsical about this crime,' he said. 'Last week we did a stolen car racket and the week before there was the Ludgate Circus drug ring. You knew where you were with that class of crime. Villains are villains. This is too middle class.'

'I know what you mean,' said Bognor, 'only for me it's almost slumming. I seem to specialize in upper class murders. I've got the last two lines of that verse you gave me.'

He recited them and Sanders laughed sardonically.

'Doesn't get me any further,' he said. 'I'm foxed.'

'I have a hunch,' said Bognor after some deliberation. He told the policeman about the blackmailing and then, contrary to caution, about the file on Milborn Port.

'So,' he concluded, 'if Milborn Port was passing on scurrilous gossip to Russian intelligence and if St John Derby knew about it then you have a classic blackmail situation.'

'Right.'

'And finally,' said Bognor, 'the worm turned. Milborn decided he'd had enough. Arranged to meet Derby late at night in the office ostensibly to hand over more cash but actually to have a show-down. Then he realizes that Anthea Morrison knew more than she should so he takes the only way out and pushes her under the tube train. Finally he decides that I'm on to him and warns me off.'

'Super,' said Sanders. 'Now try proving it.'

'That's your job.'

'Ha.' Yet again he lit a new cigarette from the final flames of the old one. 'I wonder if you have any idea how many medium built men in dark overcoats and hats and scarves there were at Blackfriars station last night. And how amazingly unobservant the British public is. Particularly when it has a train to catch.' He shrugged. 'Never mind. You keep a good eye on your colleagues. We'll smoke them out before long.'

'If they don't kill me first,' said Bognor.

He never made it to the Pepys office. When the lift reached the fifth floor he was the only passenger left in. As he started blearily to emerge on to terra firma a ladylike hand pressed him decisively on the chest and pushed him back into the lift. At the same time Molly Mortimer said cheerily, 'Time for the hair of the dog.'

'Oh no,' said Bognor, but he was too late. The antique doors clanged behind them and the Heath Robinson inspired contraption descended. Molly was immaculate. This morning's coat was suede and belted, she carried a leather shoulder bag and was smoking a Black Russian in a holder. She wore tinted glasses and a costermonger's cap in black velvet.

'You look like the thinking man's Mata Hari,' he said. 'I'm off drink.'

'Christ,' she said, peering at his wounds. 'He must have put a lot into it.' The lift came to a jangling halt at the ground floor and they had to fight their way past an incoming throng of *Globe* employees.

'It's eleven,' she said. 'A Bloody Mary will set you up.'

'No.'

'Coffee then.'

'Oh all right.' She took his elbow and propelled him

gently but decisively across the busy street whose traffic parted like the waters of the Dead Sea except for a Number Eleven bus which shaved their bottoms.

'Immigrant!' shouted Miss Mortimer, gaily.

Bognor swore under his breath. He was unhappy.

Inside the café, which was long and low, smoky and noisy, he ordered two coffees while Molly unbuttoned her coat revealing a cashmere roll neck which accentuated her breasts. They looked, Bognor thought, larger than yesterday. 'I thought your story on the Prince of Wales Own Midland Light Infantry was a very good read,' she said. 'I wasn't so happy with the Gloster Thespians. A bit flat. You look appalling.'

'I feel bloody appalling,' he hissed. 'What the hell do you mean, "he must have put a lot into it"? What do you know about it?'

She blew at the froth on her coffee. 'I do wish they wouldn't put candy floss on perfectly good coffee,' she said. 'I'm afraid I have some explaining to do.'

'It had better be good.'

'Not particularly. Does it hurt?'

'Yes, of course it bloody hurts.'

'Poor lamb.' She made a little moue and smiled. Bognor forgave her instantly. 'I'm afraid it was Willy.'

'Willy?'

'Willy Wimbledon. You met him yesterday. He's very young.'

'And you and he . . .'

She nodded. 'Not for long. But he's terribly pretty and very good at it. Anyway he hit you and I'm apologizing for him. I really am dreadfully sorry.'

'Why can't he apologize for himself?'

'He's trying to see Liberace or he would. But Granny insisted he went.'

'Liberace?'

'We missed him yesterday and Lord Wharfedale's peeved.'

'I'm sorry,' he said, passing a hand over his forehead and sucking his teeth, 'but I simply do not understand.'

'Willy thinks he's in love with me,' she said, lowering

her voice as a large thug-faced man in a sheepskin coat turned to look at them, 'and he was on his way to the flat when he saw you leaving. You may not remember but you weren't very steady on your feet and I was having to do quite a lot of propping up. Then, which again you won't remember, I rather foolishly kissed you goodnight. Not a real kiss, just a little kiss, Board of Trade officials for the use of, but enough, I'm afraid, to make poor Willy upset. Besides he'd been drinking too. He'd been to the opening of the Hilton in Oxford Street. So he waited in the alley until you came up and then he "thumped" you, as he put it.'

'Bloody hard.'

'It could have been worse. He boxed for Cambridge.'

'So bloody childish.'

'But darling, Willy *is* bloody childish. Eton and Cambridge and straight on to a national newspaper column and a title and two blues and stacks of money, how on earth could he be anything but bloody childish?' She drank coffee and looked embarrassed. Fleetingly Bognor thought she looked almost vulnerable but he let the idea pass. She was, he remembered, as hard as old boots.

'You do realize how serious this could be?'

'What? How?'

'Thumping someone in my position. An official investigating a murder.'

'Don't be pompous.'

'I'm not being pompous.' He noticed that several people were trying to eavesdrop, an inevitable hazard he supposed of having an interesting conversation in Fleet Street. 'All I'm saying is that it happened only an hour or so after a man wearing the same outfit pushed Anthea Morrison under the Richmond train at Blackfriars.'

'The same outfit?'

'Yes.'

'How do you know?'

'You forget,' he said, 'this is my job. I'm being paid to investigate murder.'

She smiled. 'Forgive me saying so but it is easy to forget.'

'All I'm saying is that we—the police and I— have our suspicions. And one of them is that the man who pushed Anthea Morrison under the underground train is the same man who punched me in the face. And if as you say the man who punched me is Viscount bloody Wimbledon then he's going to have to do more than apologize to me. He'll end up answering to a judge and jury.'

'That's ridiculous.'

'It's true.'

'But why should Willy push Anthea Morrison under a tube train? You'll be saying next that he stabbed St John with the paper knife.'

'Yes.'

'But why?'

'That's what I aim to find out.'

Most of this exchange had been carried on in a whisper but their manner and gesticulations, coupled with Bognor's strange, mutilated appearance, had provoked much interest among their fellow coffee drinkers. Bognor paid the bill and they left amid the scrutiny of all the two dozen in the café.

'What's on today?' he asked as they made a second foolhardy crossing of the street.

'Nothing much. It's always chaos without Anthea and Granny's in a panic about the Sevens on Sunday. I think you're down for the P.M. at the philatelists' convention at the Albert Hall.'

They were in the bizarre entrance hall now and once more Bognor was struck by the Wharfedale motto. 'The truth, the whole truth and nothing but the truth,' he murmured to himself, 'but someone, so help me God, is not telling it.' Aloud he said to Molly, 'The Sevens? What Sevens?'

'The *Daily Globe* Rugby Union Seven-a-side Tournament?' said Molly, putting on a fruity hurrah harry voice. 'Darling where have you been? Apart from the Expo-Brit scheme it's practically the only thing we *do* sponsor, and it's bloody awful. Beer and sweat and gale force winds and we all have to go.'

'All? Why?'

'Because the entire column is devoted to it. We do it with Expo-Brit too but that's easy because the firms taking part are sometimes moderately interesting but I can tell you it's murder trying to find enough stories about a day's rugby.'

'Murder's the word.'

She glanced at him. They were in the passage now, lino floored, cream painted with stout wooden doors leading off. They were alone.

'Honestly,' she said, 'I *am* sorry. We came looking for you when he'd told me but you'd vanished. I promise I'll make it up to you somehow.'

'You can't have looked far,' he said, disbelievingly.

'We didn't come straight away because he didn't tell me straight away. When we did all we found was a little bit of blood. We walked down to the square and one of the drivers at the rank said a man spitting blood and alcohol had just gone off in a cab. So I realized you were safe. Honestly. Mind you I'm surprised you were able to walk that far.'

'I think I crawled,' said Bognor, theatrically. 'I feel like it. Come on, we're late.'

The office was in despair. The depression had an almost physical presence like a fog. A temporary secretary, an acned plump girl in a tiny grey skirt and remedial sandals sat at Anthea Morrison's desk. Everyone else was silent, slouched over some largely imaginary chore. Empty champagne bottles, usually an apt symbol of merriment and high life, were like gate crashers at a wake, and last night's waste paper, usually conscientiously cleared first thing by Miss Morrison, still lay where it had fallen or been thrown. The mail was still unopened and secured by the thick elastic band which the messengers had put round it.

'You're late,' said Mr Gringe without looking up. 'I will not tolerate tardiness.'

Bognor looked at the thinning grey hair on top of his head, at the worry lines on his forehead and the thin anxious mouth. He wore a stiff collar—something Bognor had scarcely seen since school and a maroon cardigan under the shapeless grey jacket. It was not an appropriate costume for the job and he wasn't an appropriate person. Bogner felt sorry for him.

'I'm sorry,' he said, 'I got held up.'

'Well please don't let it happen again. These are quite exceptionally distressing times and it's important that we all pull together.' He shook his head, releasing a little flurry of dandruff and his voice trembled slightly. 'We're all very upset about what has happened,' he went on. 'I've put you down for the Prime Minister's speech at the philatelists' convention. He's speaking at twelve-thirty but I should make a point of getting there early. I'll give you some more stories to do when we've dealt with the mail.'

'Right,' said Bognor, wondering how much longer Mr Gringe would stand the strain. No wonder they called him Granny. He picked a copy of the *Globe* from the table in the centre of the office and took it to his desk.

'Good grief,' said Milborn Port, suddenly noticing Bognor's face. 'What have you done to yourself?'

'I fell downstairs,' he said thickly. Milborn was smoking a cheroot. He took it out of his mouth and raised his eyebrows.

'Looks more as if someone gave you a thump,' he said. 'Hey, Bertie, have a look at Bognor's face. You been laying into him?'

The Honourable Bertie Harris went on reading the *Financial Times*. 'Pilton's are down again,' he said. 'I think there might be a paragraph in that somewhere. What did you say, Milborn?'

'I asked if you'd seen Bognor's face?'

'No,' he drawled. 'I saw it yesterday. Has it changed?'

'Yes.'

He put down the *Financial Times* with a sigh and examined Bognor cursorily.

'Oh,' he said. 'For a moment I thought Milborn meant you'd put on a false nose or a moustache to cheer us all up. What was it? Fisticuffs?'

'I fell downstairs.'

'Oh, well,' he said, resuming his paper, 'if you don't want to tell us, don't. I wouldn't dream of prying myself. All the same I should suggest a large piece of fillet steak applied to the bruising might well assist. If you can't afford fillet rump should do.'

Bognor turned to the Samuel Pepys column and saw that Lord Wharfedale's tribute to the deceased St John Derby on their behalf was the lead item. He was glad that his typing had been so useful. Alongside it there was a photograph of the dead man and he realized that he had never before seen a picture of him. It was an interesting face now that he had the opportunity to study it, even in the hazy grey half tones of the tiny Samuel Pepys reproduction. There was a caption under it, penned presumably by Peckwater, 'St J. Derby,' it said. 'Unequalled flair.' It was a photograph which must have been taken a little while ago, judging by the darkness of the hair and the clarity of the eye. Bognor peered at it and wondered if it was a blackmailer's face. There was something about the way the nostrils flared and the mouth curved sardonically which suggested humorous dishonesty, he thought. Or was he simply being fanciful? He appeared to have a scar on his cheek below the left eye.

'Did St John Derby have a scar?' he asked the room in general.

Molly answered. 'It isn't a scar,' she said, 'it's a birthmark.'

'He always told me he'd got it duelling at Heidelberg,' said Milborn.

'Just shows how gullible you can be, dear,' said Molly, 'if you believe that. St John left school at sixteen. He never went near a university, let alone Heidelberg. Don't you remember him going on about the university of life?'

Silence. Bognor looked over to Milborn's desk and was shocked to see him dabbing at his eyes with an immense red and white polka dot handkerchief. He looked away in embarrassment and no one said anything. Presently Gringe, who had been sorting letters, started to go round the room dishing out tasks.

'Milborn,' he said when he came opposite his desk, 'Irving G. Silverberg is staying at the Hyde Park. Would you nip round and try to have a word with him?'

Milborn looked up at him blankly. Still puffy-eyed. 'Irving who?'

'G. Silverberg, the man who made *Bat Out of Hell* and *The Coffee Grinders*.'

Milborn blew his nose noisily. 'It's not quite my pigeon, old boy,' he said huskily. 'If it's all the same to you I thought I'd nip down to Sandown and take in the first three races before . . .'

'I'm awfully sorry, Milborn, but it's not the same to me.' Granny Gringe's mouth was quivering at the edges and his left eyebrow was on the blink. 'You and Bognor can share a taxi as far as the Hyde Park and then he'll take it on to the philatelists at the Albert Hall.'

'Oh all right.' Mr Port was very obviously unhappy about this assignment, 'but who is this chap Silverberger? American by the sound of it.'

'Berg—not Berger. He makes films. He's been married five times. Once twice if you follow me.'

'No.'

Gringe's eyebrow was performing quite alarmingly.

'I mean that his first and third wife were the same person. I happen to know that Lord Wharfedale is a particular fan of his films. Cuttings will tell you. I suggest you ring the library.'

'Ha!' said Milborn, wheezing. He produced an inhaler from inside his jacket and applied it to each nostril in turn. 'Oh well if you and Lord Wharfedale say so I suppose I'd better go. You'd get a much better story from Sandown.'

'I don't want a story from Sandown. I want you back here the minute you've spoken to Mr Silverberg.'

'No need to get shirty.'

Continuing on his rounds Gringe gave Bognor another job lot of stories to improve or delve into: A clandestine marriage, a regimental dinner, a suspicious shooting accident in Inverness involving a Duke and a brace of Earls, and a sale of Victorian landscapes at Bonhams.

'You and Port had better go,' he said, eyebrow now quiescent. 'We can't afford to dawdle.'

The two of them nodded at each other.

'See you in the front hall,' said Milborn. 'I'm just going for a pee.'

A few minutes later when they met downstairs Bognor was aware of a strong aroma of alcohol on Milborn's lips. Not last night's either. It was raw and fresh and very distinct. In the taxi it was confirmed when he extracted a flask from his coat and offered it to Bognor who took a token sip. Brandy.

'Have a mint,' said Milborn proffering a grubby tube of sweets with holes in the middle, 'takes away the smell.' He took one and sucked it noisily but without satisfaction.

'You ever heard of this fellow Silverberg?'

'Sort of.'

'What sort of?'

'He makes films. He's what they call larger than life,' said Bognor. 'Big broad accent. Big broad broads.' He smirked. 'That's rather good,' he said. 'Nice pun.'

'Ghastly pun,' said Port crunching his mint noisily and beginning to smell like crème de menthe. 'Didn't he have a horse called Coffeegrinder which ran in the Laurel?'

'I wouldn't know.'

'I think that's him.' He pulled out the loud handkerchief and blew into it. 'I'm afraid I'm rather upset,' he said unnecessarily.

'I can understand,' said Bognor.

'Two going just like that,' he said gazing out at Simpsons in the Strand. 'It makes you think. I'm fifty-three.'

'You don't look it,' said Bognor, thinking he looked at least ten years older.

'Kind of you to say so. How are you enjoying life on the Diary?'

'It's certainly eventful.'

'Better than Winnipeg I should think.'

'Yes.'

'Finding it difficult?'

'Quite.'

'Tell you what then, have another drink,' he gave Bognor the flask and he took another tiny tot. 'You've got a few minutes to spare. You stop off at the Hyde Park with me and I'll show you how it's done. You might pick up a thing or two.'

'That would be very helpful,' said Bognor wondering how it was done and guessing that it would not be done with any great flair. 'Cold isn't it?'

'Pretty parky.' Mr Port slapped his hands together. He was wearing an overcoat, and it was dark, like most overcoats. He also had a Paisley scarf round his neck. But no hat.

'I suppose it would make sense to wear a hat in this sort of weather,' said Bognor, lamely. Speech was still an effort and so was original thought.

'Always wear a hat at the races,' said Milborn as their vehicle emerged from the underpass into Knightsbridge, 'but never in the office or on jobs in London. You can wear a hat on the way into the office and you can wear a hat on the way out of the office. But not in between. That's etiquette.'

'And do you?'

'Wear a hat? On those occasions, yes.'

'What sort of hat?'

'What a funny fellow you are,' said Milborn, giving

the impression that he found nothing remotely amusing about his companion. 'Trilby usually. I buy them from Lock's.'

The taxi drew up at the Hyde Park Hotel and a liveried commissionaire opened the door. As he emerged Milborn hastily patted all his most obvious pockets. 'Drat,' he said, 'I've come out without any change. Do you mind obliging, old boy? I'll do the next one.' Bognor paid off the driver and the two went inside.

Milborn wasted no time. 'Now you watch this,' he said sotto voce and advanced flamboyantly on the reception desk. 'Irving G. Silverberg,' he said loudly. Not as a question but as a statement of fact.

'I beg your pardon, sir.'

'Irving G. Silverberg, I have an appointment.'

'You have an appointment with Mr Silverberg, sir?'

'That's what I said.'

'What name is it, sir?'

'Sir Milborn Port.'

Bognor sucked his teeth. He had never heard the papal baronetcy invoked before.

'One moment, Sir Milborn.' The clerk consulted papers and returned. 'I'm very sorry, your name doesn't seem to appear on Mr Silverberg's list and I don't believe Mr Silverberg is in the hotel at this precise moment.'

Milborn frowned. 'That's most peculiar,' he said. 'My secretary arranged it only this morning.'

The clerk shrugged and waved his arms in a gesture of helplessness.

'Ah well,' said Milborn, 'would you please tell Mr Silverberg that I shall be waiting for him in the bar.' With which he turned on his heel and headed unerringly in the direction of the drink.

'It didn't seem to work,' said Bognor, unimpressed.

'Haven't started yet,' said Milborn. He summoned a waiter and ordered a bottle of Pommery. 'If he doesn't come soon,' he said, 'I shall charge it to his account.' Bognor looked at his watch.

'I'll have to go in a second,' he said. 'If I'm going to get to the Albert Hall in time for the Prime Minister.'

'Wait a second,' he said. 'I bet it works. Just watch.'

The Pommery arrived and the seconds ticked away becoming minutes when after only half a glass had been consumed a young man in rimless glasses and a Madison Avenue suit approached the table.

'Round one to us,' whispered Milborn.

'Sir Milborn Port?' enquired rimless glasses.

'Exactly,' said Milborn. 'Will you join us? This is Simon Bognor.'

'Erwin Schumacher,' said the young man, 'Mr Silverberg's personal assistant. I'd be happy to, gentlemen.'

Another glass was brought and to Bognor's surprise Milborn began to talk about racing, a subject about which Mr Schumacher seemed quite ignorant.

After a while both Bognor and it seemed to him Mr Schumacher, became increasingly perplexed. Milborn was talking about American bloodlines when Bognor decided it was time to make an excuse and leave.

'I'm afraid I have to go and see the Prime Minister,' he said, truthfully and he hoped tactfully. Milborn looked appreciative, Mr Schumacher still more bewildered.

The philatelists had made no real provision for the hordes of journalists who descended on their convention that morning. In view of the fact that it was their hundredth anniversary and because it was known that the Prime Minister had a notable private collection himself it had seemed apposite to extend an invitation. The stamp collectors, in their innocence, had assumed that the Prime Minister might make a speech about stamps. They had reckoned without the usual winter fuel crisis coupled with the recurring general economic crisis, the annual January confrontation between the government and the Trade Unions and the crisis of confidence in the government in general and the Prime Minister in particular which all this implied.

The Prime Minister had let it be known that he

would be using the hundredth anniversary convention of the world's philatelists to make an important speech. For this reason by the time Bognor arrived the solitary spinster who had been delegated to look after the press and who had been expecting nothing more than the odd correspondent of one of the specialist stamp magazines was swamped, inundated, distraught and utterly at a loss. When Bognor produced his press pass she could no more than point helplessly towards the stairs which led into the depths. Bognor took them and soon found himself in a dingy ill-lit passageway from which he could hear a flat nasal voice droning seemingly a long way off. He opened a door on his left from which the noise appeared to be coming, walked up half a dozen steps, peered over a parapet and found himself within a few yards of the guest of honour.

Bognor was not particularly impressed by the Prime Minister. He listened briefly and then let the old familiar phrases bounce off him unheeded. He was dimly aware of 'will not be held to ransom', 'pernicious sectarian influences', 'pulling together in a United Britain' and 'we are beating inflation'. The stamp collectors, of whom there were several thousand, looked bored rigid, but the press who were sprawled across the rows to Bognor's immediate left were writing assiduously. Their photographers were gathered underneath the rostrum hung about with an armoury of cameras and lenses which they occasionally raised to eye level.

Bognor moved to an empty seat among some murmured 'Ssssh' sounds from his colleagues and picked up a stencilled copy of the premier's speech. He perused it sceptically, wondering why other journalists took notes when it was all typed out for them and looked for references to stamps. He found a joke about 'Having done my stamp duty', and a reference to rubber stamps and bureaucracy of whose humorous intention he was unsure. There was also a reference almost a paragraph long to the greatly improved design of British stamps and the imaginative subjects depicted on them. The Royal wedding stamps were cited in evidence and he said that we had come a long way since the Penny Black. All this Bognor underlined for use in his story. Then he tried to assimilate some atmosphere. This he knew he needed to give 'colour' to his story. He had been told that this was an important element.

He scanned the hall not knowing quite what he was looking for. Not much point in describing the interior of the Albert Hall since most people had seen it on television. He supposed he should include some eminent philatelists but he had no idea what an eminent philatelist looked like. Desperately he peered about him, praying for something to attract his attention, something which would keep Granny Gringe happy. Then his eyes lit on a half familiar figure scribbling frenziedly on to a foolscap pad. It looked like Spencer Nugent of Magdalen. He racked his memory. Spencer had edited *Isis* and gone into journalism. He had noticed his name somewhere recently. Political editor of the *Daily News*? He had an idea that was it but couldn't be sure. Then his attention was diverted as the Prime Minister reached the joke about stamp duty. It was near the bottom of the final page and that meant peroration time. The joke attracted only thin applause, though the Prime Minister laughed immoderately before putting on the 'weighty matters' face and making a final appeal to the innate patriotism of the philately fraternity. After he'd finished he found that he'd scrawled 'Balls', in huge letters across the typescript.

'Well,' he muttered, 'it was balls.'

As he was leaving he noticed Spencer Nugent still sitting in his red velvet seat examining his notes. He decided to accost him. It was years since they'd seen each other but at university they had been close, if not friends, at least close acquaintances.

He struggled past the outgoing philatelists and journalists and accosted him. Spencer turned and stared through him blankly without a shadow of recognition.

'Bognor,' said Bognor. 'You remember. Bognor.'

'God,' said Spencer, rising in a flurry of paper and

holding out his hand, 'Simon Bognor. Good God alive. Long time no see. What the hell are you doing here?'

'I'm covering it for the *Globe*.' The phrase tripped off his tongue glibly. He was rather pleased with it.

'I thought you went into the Post Office.'

'Board of Trade actually.'

'Oh well, Post Office, Board of Trade, what the hell. But why the defection?' Spencer looked prosperous and smooth as ever. He had always been outrageously smooth, always giving sherry parties for dons and spending his week-ends in London.

'Defection?'

'To the *Globe*.'

'Oh,' Bognor blushed. 'Felt like a change,' he said. 'I was getting bored with the Board of Trade.'

'I can imagine.' Spencer grinned. He had a contrived grin. Always had. He thought it was infectious. 'Are you lunching?'

'No.'

'Then let's lunch. At my club?'

It was what Bognor had been hoping for, though he feigned surprise and embarrassment. Spencer said he'd been going there anyway. It was where he got all his best stories.

'By the way, old boy,' he said as they emerged blinking into daylight, 'forgive my asking but you don't always look like that, do you? I mean it's a temporary defect, isn't it?' The sun was shining for the first time for days. The sky was crisp pale Cambridge blue and the gaunt angles of the Albert Memorial were stark in silhouette.

'I fell downstairs,' said Bognor. 'I hope it's temporary. It hurts.'

Spencer smiled. 'I should take more care if I were you,' he said. 'There seems to be a sudden distressing tendency for people on your paper to start dropping down dead.'

'Yes,' said Bognor.

They lunched at Pring's just off Piccadilly, certainly

the most expensive and arguably the most exclusive club in London. Bognor commented in genuine envy.

'My father-in-law saw to it,' said Spencer, shovelling potted shrimps on to a piece of soggy toast. 'Marvellous for Tory gossip of course. No Socialists. Well, Socialist peers if they're hereditary and of course Marxists.'

'Marxists?'

'Marxists are perfectly respectable. You know that. And we have a Liberal.'

For the first half of the meal they discussed Oxford and played 'whatever happened to?' Then Spencer described his career so far which had involved an ascent which was just short of spectacular and therefore more likely to continue.

'Doesn't pay to look flashy,' he said, rejecting a soggy sprout, 'as you'll discover. They don't like brains and they don't like graduates. Oxford can be death. I keep very quiet about it and say I was at school in Yorkshire. It sounds suitably working class.'

They had arrived at the Stilton when Spencer nodded an acknowledgement towards the dining-room door. Bognor half turned and saw two young middle-aged men in Savile Row suiting. One of them was Bertie Harris who favoured Bognor with a glacial smile which implied that Bognor was social climbing. At least it implied it to Bognor who was sensitive to allegations of snobbery, genuine or false.

'I was forgetting,' said Spencer. 'Harris is filling in time on the Pepys Show, isn't he?'

'Yes. Who's the other one?'

'Elliston Gravelle.'

'What, Lord Grampian's son?'

'Yes. He's our Managing Director. I can't think why Wharfedale doesn't give Bertie Harris more responsibility like that. He's perfectly competent. Just not interested.'

The two under discussion sat at a table in a window where Bognor and Spencer Nugent were able to watch without appearing inquisitive. They were markedly similar in appearance though there was a suggestion of effete languor, a hint of debauchery about Bertie which was much less pronounced in Elliston.

'Ambitious lad, our Elliston,' said Spencer. 'I think he has designs on the *Globe* Group.'

'Oh. That's not possible, surely?'

'Not while old Wharfedale's alive I grant you, but I have a feeling that when he's gone to God Bertie might be as happy looking after the farms and playing a bit of polo. Winter in St Moritz, summer on the Costa Smeralda, autumn on the moors, that would just about suit Bertie.'

'Why doesn't he do that now then?'

'Port?' Bognor who was restored to hazy equilibrium by the club claret agreed. 'Daddy holds the purse strings,' said Spencer. 'And Daddy will make his Bertie into a professional newspaperman or die in the attempt. My personal view is that he'll die in the attempt.'

'Could the *News* take over the *Globe*? I thought they sold fewer copies.'

'They do but the *News* has greater assets. It's a richer organization. Still, nothing will happen till the old men give up the ghost. They can't stand each other.'

'So they don't approve?'

Bognor liked port. He rolled it round his mouth and helped himself to another biscuit.

'How well do you know Elliston Gravelle?' he asked.

'Not socially. Well, we might have a drink in here. Occasionally at week-ends. He's a first rate shot. I saw him get a woodcock once in a force seven gale and hail, after lighting up time. I didn't even know there was a bird there. But I see a fair bit of him in the office. As political editor I'm nominally a departmental head, so I have what's laughingly known as "access" to him.'

'If Wharfedale thought Bertie Harris might sell out his interests after he succeeded what would he do?'

Spencer Nugent looked across to Harris and Gravelle who were engrossed in serious talk. 'They look like conspirators, don't they?' he ventured, 'but they're probably discussing form or women. They both have something of a reputation as ladies' men. I gather they were notorious at the House.' He sipped port. 'But in answer to your question. Two things. First I should think Wharfedale has made Bertie swear in blood that he will hang on to the *Globe* come hell or high water. Second I should imagine that if he had serious doubts he would probably disinherit. There are nephews who could take over. It's unlikely though.'

Bognor sucked his teeth and wondered if it would be permissible to start making lists in the members' dining room at Pring's. Almost certainly not, he decided. Sort of thing a fellow would be blackballed for. Worse than cheating at cards.

'But,' he persisted, 'you really think it's conceivable that Bertie Harris might eventually sell the family newspaper to his most deadly rival?'

'He's not a deadly rival of Elliston's,' said Spencer. 'They're old muckers. It's the fathers who are the deadly rivals.' He leant forward across the heavy silver plate pepper and salt, and lowered his voice.

'I've heard it said that it's in writing already.'

'What?'

'An agreement to merge the two groups when they've both inherited.'

'Merge?'

'Polite formula. Bertie would stay on as nominal vice chairman or some such rubbish and he'd get a lot of money.'

'How sure are you about this?'

'I'm not sure, but I've heard things. My contacts are pretty good. Anyway why are you so keen to know? You don't have to worry. When I'm Editor of the *News of the Globe* or whatever they're going to call it I'll make sure you're sitting pretty.'

They changed the subject to the awfulness of the Prime Minister and his speech and shortly afterwards returned to Fleet Street.

6

As he was about to open the door of the Samuel Pepys office Bognor was aware of noise within. Men's voices were raised in heated altercation. Bognor heard the rumble of obscene expletives from a voice he judged through the stout timbers of the door to be that of Milborn Port, while in answer the more tremulous whining tones of Eric Gringe replied with sentences which sounded just as rude. Bognor hesitated and then decided to risk the inevitable unpleasantness. He tempered the abruptness of his entrance by knocking first.

Inside he found that the effect of rage had been to send Milborn scarlet while the equally choleric Granny Gringe had had all the colour drained from him so that he was pallid to the point of yellowness.

'Aha,' said Milborn, 'Bognor will confirm it, you whited sepulchre. Tell him, Bognor. Just tell him.' The stench of alcoholic mint was unbearable.

'Tell him what?' Bognor was genuinely unaware of what it could possibly be that he was supposed to tell.

'There is nothing you can possibly tell which will alter the obvious and distressing fact that he is as drunk . . . as drunk.' Mr Gringe was evidently unable to find anything which could possibly be as drunk as Mr Port . . . '. . . as a newt,' he ended finally, the word rasping from his pursed lips with inapposite venom.

'You said he owned horses, you little wet,' shouted Milborn, his eyes rolling, 'and he's never been near a horse in his life. He's allergic to them.'

'I said nothing about horses, I said he made films.'

'You said he owned Coffeegrinder.'

'I said he made a film called *The Coffee Grinders*.'

'Balls!'

'Lies!'

Bognor, mesmerized by this performance, snapped

out of his trance. 'Are we talking about Mr Silverberg?' he asked.

'Yes,' they agreed hoarsely. He had the impression that the row had been going on for some time. Both men seemed near exhaustion.

'Well, what do you want me to tell you?' he asked meekly and in as polite and soft a voice as was possible through his still livid lips and after a respectable quantity of Pring's claret and port.

'What happened?' said Gringe, with a prissy air of imminent triumph. 'Just tell me what happened. That's all I need to know. Then I'll break you, Port. I'll break you.' Mr Gringe looked incapable of breaking anyone. His fury made him seem more frail and put upon than ever and Bognor saw to his dismay that his eyebrow had again gone out of control.

'Nothing much to tell,' said Bognor, wondering how much would be tactful and if he was going to take sides whose side it would be most politic to be on. 'We arrived at the Hyde Park Hotel and Milborn asked for Mr Silverberg and the clerk said he didn't think Mr Silverberg was in so Milborn said he'd wait in the bar and then Mr Silverberg's assistant turned up and joined us and then I had to leave for the Albert Hall.'

'That's not all . . . that's not all,' screamed Gringe, enraged. 'What name did he give. He gave a false name.'

'He gave the name Milborn Port,' said Bognor.

'But he prefixed it. He prefixed it.'

'Yes,' conceded Bognor reluctantly, 'he did say "Sir Milborn Port" .'

'Liar!' shouted Gringe. 'Imbecile! Impostor!'

'I'm entitled to it,' Milborn bellowed back. 'It's my name damn you. *Sir* Milborn Port. I'm the fourteenth baronet.'

'*Papal* baronet!' Mr Gringe spat it out in such a way that papal became as derogatory a word as the 'paper' in 'paper tiger'.

'Nothing wrong with that.'

'Honestly,' said Bognor, 'I don't see that it matters.

After all what's in a name? Sticks and stones may break your bones, but . . .' He was sadly aware that he was being fatuous.

'That's not all,' said Gringe. 'Nothing like all. That's only the beginning. In all my years of journalism I have never experienced such deceit.'

'All your years of journalism, my arse. You don't begin to be a journalist. You've never been further than bloody Bromley. You've spent all your years of journalism sitting in this office doing bugger all while the rest of us go out and get the stories and do the real work.'

'Gentlemen, really,' Bognor attempted a second intercession, 'I still don't know what happened.'

'Perfectly simple,' said Milborn, 'you saw the first bit. There I was sitting in the bar chatting up Silverberg's assistant, all nice and cosy, and suddenly I realize that not only does he not know the first thing about horses but nor does Silverberg. So he starts to get shirty and tries to leave without paying.'

'Without paying?'

'He'd drunk half the champagne and the little bugger wouldn't even pay his share. So there was a row. All because this incompetent granny here gave me a totally wrong briefing.'

Mr Gringe interrupted. 'I was sitting here trying to work under exceptionally difficult circumstances when the telephone rang and the hotel manager said that a man purporting to be a member of my staff was making a scene in the bar. I need hardly say that I knew immediately to whom he was referring.'

'Not surprising since you'd sent me there in the first place.'

Mr Gringe ignored the remark. 'I naturally went straight to the hotel, leaving the office unmanned, and managed to settle the affair as amicably as possible. I very much hope that no official complaint is made to Lord Wharfedale. You owe me eight pounds for the champagne and the broken ash tray.'

'You can't have it. You should never have paid. It's your own bloody fault.'

'In that case I shall dock it from your expenses.'

'You'll do nothing of the kind.'

'We all know why you were brought home from Russia. You'll be finished after this.'

At the mention of Russia Milborn seemed to subside. He sat down heavily and without any thought of the others pulled the flask from his coat and drank noisily from it. Then he wiped his mouth and replaced the cap before glancing up at Gringe, who was staring down at him with an expression of mixed anger, contempt and incredulity.

'This is beyond belief,' he said eventually.

'Oh for God's sake, you prissy old puritan, give over,' said Milborn, wearily. 'I've had about as much as I can take.'

'You most certainly have,' exclaimed Gringe. He was now, Bognor realized, incensed beyond anything that had gone earlier. Something had snapped inside him. With a sudden lunge he made a grab at the flask, took Milborn by surprise and succeeded in making off with it. He scuttled back to his desk holding the offending object at arm's length and slammed it into a drawer. He then turned a key on it and sat back with a smirk of manic triumph on his face, rather as if he had succeeded in ensnaring and caging some dangerous wild animal. Throughout this Bognor had remained gaping, open-mouthed, but now with a realization that someone had to control the situation, he tried for a third time to restore sanity. He was too late.

The theft of his alcohol re-galvanized Milborn. Gringe's grab had caught him unprepared and it took him a moment to realize that a crime had been committed. Then just as Gringe was looking at his smuggest with the offending alcohol safely under lock and key, Port let out a stentorian bellow which would have done credit to a Guards Drill Sergeant:

'GIVE ME BACK MY BLOODY BOOZE!'

'I shall not,' said Gringe, evidently feeling himself in

the superior position. Very deliberately he put the key in his trouser pocket. 'You may have it back after work but not until. From now on there will be sobriety in this office. I have had enough of this persistent drunkenness.' Bognor felt he was being unwise. It seemed to him that Gringe's position was more precarious than it might seem to him. And so it immediately transpired.

With another bellow, this time totally incoherent, Milborn Port, looking every inch the wronged fourteenth baronet, papal or not, strode towards his boss. Too late Eric Gringe realized his danger. Too late he tried to temporize. Too late he called to Bognor for help. In a trice 'Sir' Milborn had grabbed the maroon cardigan by the shoulders and hauled the helpless wearer to his feet, then steadying his target with his left hand he took a mighty swipe with his right and let go. Mr Gringe crumpled and fell back into his chair. His attacker eyed him and then wordlessly felt in the trouser pocket, fetched out the key, unlocked the drawer and retrieved his possession. He then went to the coat hooks, removed his overcoat which he put over one arm and a trilby hat which he jammed jauntily on the back of his head.

'Goodbye,' he said to Bognor. 'See you at the Sevens.' And then he was gone.

No sooner had he done so than Bertie Harris entered.

'Just passed Milborn on his way out,' he said jauntily, 'looking pleased with himself in a thunderously boozed fashion. What's . . . ah.' He noticed Mr Gringe who was just beginning to stir groggily in his chair. 'I see,' said Mr Harris. 'That's what he was so pleased about.'

Mr Gringe was regaining consciousness steadily. The blow had caught him on the side of his face and it had, Bognor reckoned, been its shock and surprise rather than strength which had caused him to pass out. At any rate it did not look as if there was any real reason to worry about his health despite the low whine he was now emitting and the cautious and aggrieved way in which he was exploring his face with tentative fingers.

Bertie Harris said nothing but looked inquiringly.

'There was a row over an interview with Irving G. Silverberg. Milborn cocked it up.'

'The race horse owner,' said Bertie authoritatively.

'No. That was the trouble. The film producer. Milborn was certain he was a race horse owner and behaved accordingly and one way and another the results were disastrous. Granny had to go and rescue him from the Hyde Park Hotel *and* cough up for a bottle of Pommery and a broken ash tray.'

They both stared at the injured party.

'Let's give him a lift,' said Bertie and together they gently hauled him up and arranged him comfortably in his chair.

'Don't suppose he's used to it,' said Bertie. He glanced at Bognor's still puffy appearance and rubbed his jaw reflectively. 'There seems to be a quite terrifying rise in the incidence of violent assault around these offices,' he said. 'I didn't know you were a member of Pring's.'

'I'm not,' said Bognor. 'I was taken there by Spencer Nugent.'

'I see. Elliston Gravelle says he's one of his bright young men. I always feel there's something essentially unsound in his writing, but then I don't pretend to an expert knowledge.'

'I knew him at Oxford.'

'How curious. Elliston and I were at Oxford. I'd never thought of Pring's as an extension to the Grid.'

'Err . . .' A long dry rasping entreaty came from the semi-comatose figure of Eric Gringe. Both men bent down to listen. 'Water,' said Bognor, after straining for a moment. 'He wants water.'

Bertie Harris said he would fetch some from the iced water machine outside the Editor's office and left Bognor to Mr Gringe and his thoughts. Bognor's thoughts were once more confused. He remembered the right hook which Milborn had used. It had been a useful punch. Then he closed his eyes and tried to recall last night. He wished he hadn't been so drunk. It seemed to him that his punch was not unlike the one that had poleaxed Gringe. And yet one punch was very much like another. He opened his eyes and saw Gringe staring at him balefully.

'I . . . er . . .' he murmured but Bognor put a finger to his lips and said 'Shhhh'. 'I wouldn't try to talk yet,' he added. 'It's too painful. Wait till you've got your water.' Then he returned to his theories. If it had been Milborn who hit him last night why had Molly confessed on Willy Wimbledon's behalf? It suggested conspiracy. Perhaps it had been Milborn and the Wimbledon story was a decoy. To suggest that the hot-headed Viscount had struck him for reasons of sexual jealousy was better than admitting that Milborn had misguidedly attacked him in an effort to warn him away from meddling in murder. He sighed. Perhaps it was just coincidence. The papal baronet's motive for attacking Gringe was obvious enough even if it was palpably silly. The Viscount's for hitting him was equally absurd but just as plausible. Given the tightening tension of the atmosphere it was perhaps not unnatural for people to start laying into each other. The strain was just too much for them all.

Bertie Harris came back with the iced water, closely followed by Molly Mortimer, Wimbledon and the temporary secretary. Bognor gave them a quick résumé while Bertie administered water.

'Brandy would be better,' said Molly.

Gringe went a whiter shade of pale and Bognor made as if to kick her shins.

'I don't think alcohol is a safe or constructive topic of conversation,' said Bertie, holding the glass to Gringe's lips. 'It would help if you all sat down at your desks. There's no point in crowding the poor fellow.'

Bognor and the others recognized the authority in Harris's voice and did as they were told. Half-heartedly he toiled with the stories Gringe had given him earlier and wrote a leaden account of the Prime Minister's speech to the philatelists, highlighting the ponderous quip about 'Stamp Duty' and suggesting the same words as the headline. His heart was not in it. Out of the corner of his eye he watched Gringe regain consciousness and composure. When he had finally done so Bertie Harris whispered to him almost fiercely with a great deal of finger wagging. Then he turned to the rest of them and said, 'I don't think Eric is in any state to stay on for the rest of this afternoon so I've asked him to go home and get a decent sleep. We can cope quite adequately on our own.' Slightly to Bognor's surprise Mr Gringe did not demur. There was now a nasty pink patch where he'd been punched but otherwise he was still deathly pale. Bognor guessed it was more than the physical pain that was disconcerting him. He too must be wondering about Milborn. If he could knock out one boss for the confiscation of a hip flask, why couldn't he stab another with a paper knife for a similarly paltry reason? Or push a secretary under a tube train? To Bognor that seemed less likely. There was a coldness about that crime, if crime it was, which did not tie in with Milborn Port's boozy brand of aggression. Nevertheless it didn't look good. If St John Derby had been blackmailing him over the Russians then ...

'I say, have you finished?' It was Viscount Wimbledon, a great deal more diffident than he had been under the Chelsea lamp-post the night before.

'Yes actually.' Bognor, despite his lack of concentration, had just completed a colourful description of the forthcoming Regimental Dinner of the 13th/39th Queen's Cuirassiers, nicknamed the Pink and Purples. He had dwelt lovingly on the Regiment's traditions and silver, which were, of course, intimately connected and had laid ghoulish emphasis on the jewel encrusted human skull acquired during the Abyssinian campaign from the Emperor Theodore. It was his fifth story and he felt he had acquitted himself well.

'I'm awfully sorry about last night,' said the Viscount. 'I just wanted to apologize. It was all a mistake.'

'Rather a painful mistake.'

'Yes I'm really extremely sorry. I'm afraid I was rather over-emotional and I didn't realize quite who you were.'

'Oh.' Bognor couldn't think of anything satisfactory to say. Wimbledon looked embarrassed and contrite and he had apologized. The convention was to thank him for apologizing but Bognor's mouth still ached too much for that. Besides he *had* hit him. At least that was what he was saying and Bognor wasn't in the mood to let him off lightly.

'Can I buy you a drink after work?' he asked.

Bognor wondered what Molly Mortimer saw in him. Youth and fitness, he supposed. He was callow but he still had his beauty.

'It's very kind of you,' he said, 'but I'm still awash with the excesses of yesterday. Perhaps on Sunday at the Sevens?'

'It would have to be afterwards I'm afraid. Or at least after we're knocked out. Drinking before matches is frowned on. Ridiculous really when you think how much most of the players will have had the night before.'

'I didn't realize you were playing. I thought cricket was your game—apart from boxing. Surely they don't play rugger at Eton?'

The young man smiled and Bognor got a clear and unpleasing idea of why Molly fancied him. The teeth were even and unblemished and the lines at the mouth and eyes crinkled attractively and then disappeared as if by magic, the moment his face went back into repose.

'Not very well but we do play a bit now and I played for my college at Cambridge.'

'Not for the University? I got the impression you played for the University at whatever you tried.'

The plastically attractive face clouded for a moment. 'My defence was described as suspect,' he said, 'also they weren't keen on my pedigree. Silly, but there's a strong rugby mafia and they don't like interlopers.'

Bognor allowed himself a complacent little smile. He

knew enough about rugger to realize that Viscount Wimbledon hadn't got any further with it because he was regarded as a coward. Odd for someone who boxed as well as he did but, he reflected, there is the world of difference between deploying pugilistic skill with an opponent of similar size but lesser ability, and having to knock over some muscular oaf of seventeen stone who is running straight towards you. Viscount Wimbledom was obviously a man who did not like getting his knees muddy.

'Who are you playing for?'

'The Terrapins, actually.'

Odd, thought Bognor how a particular sort of person managed to say 'actually' so often, particularly when showing off. The Terrapins were very smart, mostly former Oxbridge blues, though their playing reputation was less gilded than in former times.

'Where are you playing?'

'Fly half, actually.'

That followed. Fly half was the flash position where you could indulge your fancy footwork. Bognor himself, who had not played since school, used to be a hooker. That meant being constantly anonymous, grinding along in the middle of a sweaty mass of heaving humanity and having your shins hacked. Men like him had scant regard for the elegant individuals who pranced about outside the scrum doing none of the work and getting all the glory.

'Good luck then.' He caught the cynical inflection in his voice and realized with a frisson of self-knowledge that he was jealous. He attempted to remedy it. 'I really do hope you do well. Are London Welsh playing?'

The Viscount nodded. 'They're favourites.'

'They would be,' said Bognor, 'still it can pay to be underdogs . . . and by the way . . . about last night. No hard feelings.' He put out a hand for shaking, privately appalled that he should lapse into such clichéd behaviour. Nonetheless he felt it was what Wimbledon wanted and indeed he responded with enthusiasm, pumping his hand up and down as if an enormous responsibility had been removed.

'Thanks,' he said. 'That's awfully good of you. I really do appreciate it. I'll buy you a pint on Sunday, win or lose.'

'Win or lose,' said Bognor.

The rump of the column's staff with no St John Derby, no Eric Gringe, no Milborn Port, and no Anthea Morrison produced a turgid performance. Bognor's offerings, which could hardly be said to scintillate were the lightest and most entertaining in a dull day. Bertie Harris commented on the fact as he dismissed them, chiding the others while accepting some responsibility himself. It was tacitly acknowledged on all sides that to have produced a column at all under the amazingly distressing and difficult circumstances which prevailed, was a formidable achievement. The Sunday Sevens were awaited with some trepidation but meanwhile Saturday was a day of rest.

Bognor went home by bus since the London underground system, still 'working to rule', was now going so slow that forward motion was barely discernible. His evening newspaper headlined the Prime Minister's speech to the philatelists, describing it as 'a back to the wall message of grim defiance'. Elsewhere the news was all of rising prices and lowering morale and monotonous predictions of gloom and doom. He read the report of the premier's speech and noted that no reference was made to the joke about stamp duty nor to anything in any way connected with philately. Poor old philatelists, he thought and sighed with feeling. It was only two days since he had started as a reporter on the Pepys column and yet already he felt like a hardened professional.

The bus was crawling almost as slowly as the underground trains. Faced with train strikes all London seemed to have taken to its cars and buses and Bognor was acutely conscious of the lack of morale which the press described. No one even had the enthusiasm left to complain. Instead the other passengers sat staring blankly into space or their papers, their breath hanging on the cold air like smoke. The prevailing pessimism affected him. There was, he told himself morosely, enough to be pessimistic about without a national fit of depression to make it worse. He didn't suppose anybody else on the freezing double-decker had been hit on the mouth and banged the back of their head on a lamp-post, been witness to another knock-out, and involved, however vicariously, in two killings. The use of the word vicariously reminded him of the feeble pun of yesterday. The trouble was that this was no longer a vicarious experience. He was, willy nilly, involved, and he had a sneaking, scaring suspicion that the more he got involved the more likely it was that he would be the next corpse.

When, an hour and a half later, he got home he was in a foul, frustrated mood which he was determined to expunge.

'I'm late but I'm sober,' he said to Monica, 'and it doesn't hurt quite as much and I'm not going to think about murders or newspapers until the morning.'

Monica seemed to think this was a reasonable resolution. 'I was afraid you were going to spend the evening making lists,' she said. It was an apprehension founded on past history. Whenever an investigation reached the stage of incomprehensible complexity which his investigations inevitably reached, he found solace in pencil and paper. The simple writing down of names and facts and theories was soothing. It also ordered his jumbled mind, eliminating some of the red herrings and producing patterns where previously there had been only chaos. Best of all it gave him a sense, however spurious, of accomplishing something. It was, he knew, time for some conscientious listmaking.

'Tomorrow,' he said. 'Tomorrow I'll make lists and you can help me. We'll drive somewhere and find a pub and go for a walk and we'll make lists. Tonight I want to make love not lists.'

She smiled. She had taken trouble with her hair and

her make-up and her clothes and she looked desirable. Not, he knew, in the same way as Molly Mortimer. Cosier, less dangerous, and that was what he needed.

'I'm glad you're feeling up to it,' she said, 'you must be better. But later. I've made a curry.'

He had a bath and then the curry, which was spicy with cardamom and coriander, and only then did they go to bed. Their lovemaking was slow and methodical and quite without unorthodoxy of any kind. It relaxed him so that at 8 A.M. when the telephone rang he was almost ready for it. For once it wasn't Parkinson.

'Sanders here, Mr Bognor.'

'Oh for heaven's sake please call me Simon.'

A pause, then: 'I assume you're still interested in the case?'

'Why?'

'I have an impression people are beginning to be nervous. Your Minister's been making trouble with the Commissioner.'

'Should know better,' said Bognor, feeling on top of the situation. 'I'm still interested. Power nil. Interest considerable. You know the score. I'll play ball with you, if . . .'

'OK. I thought you might be interested to hear we've had the results of the post mortem on Anthea Morrison.'

Bognor wasn't in the least interested. It was perfectly clear that she had died as the result of falling from the westbound platform at Blackfriars station. No autopsy could say who pushed her. However he played ball. 'That's very kind of you. What did it say?'

'She was pregnant.'

'Pregnant?'

'Pregnant.'

Bognor scratched the back of his head and found the bump left by the lamp-post. It hurt. 'Sorry,' he said, 'but does that help us?'

'That's what I'm asking you. It seems she was about three months gone. I've made some enquiries. Her mother knew nothing about a boy friend or lover and she was a devout Catholic.'

'You're suggesting she was murdered because she was pregnant?'

'I'm not suggesting anything except that her pregnancy could be a murder motive.'

'Or suicide?'

'You said it,' said Sanders.

'Was that all?' asked Bognor.

'I should have thought it was enough. Do you know who was having an affair with her?'

'No idea. Not St John Derby.' That would be a neat solution. A lovers' tiff at the office, a passionate stabbing, followed by a desolated suicide, bearing his child. However on the strength of what he knew and what had been suggested it seemed implausible.

'Did you find anything interesting in St John's papers?' asked Bognor. 'Letters, photographs?'

The policeman laughed. 'You do me an injustice,' he said. 'I would have told you. Unless your taste runs to tasteful photographs of young men artistically posed in the nude. Or a useful collection of books on bridge and a complete set of *Wisden's Cricketers' Almanack*. But nothing to incriminate anybody else.'

'That's funny. Could you have missed anything?'

'It's possible. Unlikely but possible.'

'Would you mind if I went and had a peep for myself? I'm not doubting your thoroughness but it might help me to get a clearer picture of what the old boy was like. Besides I'd like to look at the *Wisdens*.'

He could almost feel Sanders deliberating. Then he said, 'I don't see why not, but for Christ's sake don't let anyone catch you. And keep quiet about it. As I said I have a nasty feeling there's a row brewing and I don't want the Commissioner on my back. I'll drop the keys round to you myself if you give me the address.'

Bognor said he was driving out of town and wouldn't be home till mid-afternoon. Sanders claimed an appointment in St John's Wood just before lunch and promised to post the keys through Bognor's letter-

box on his way there. They could be handed back on
Monday when Sanders wanted to return to the *Globe*
for more questioning and a thorough examination of
the back staircases.

'How odd,' said Bognor, when he put the phone
down. 'Now who would have made the girl pregnant?
And why, in this day and age?' He put an arm across
the bed and patted Monica's bottom. 'You never get
pregnant.'

'Hope not,' she said dozily.

'Because you take your pills.'

' 'S'right.'

'And so you'd only get pregnant if you were careless.'

'Careless or Catholic. Why? Are you making lists?

Bognor lay back and looked at the ceiling which was
beginning to peel. There was a cobweb in the corner he
hadn't noticed before and the first signs of a crack in
the plaster. 'Sort of,' he said.

'Why?' She was awake now, still creased with sleep
and less appetizing without make-up. Her eyes seemed
to have shrunk. He told her about Anthea Morrison.

'So,' he asked finally, 'are we to believe that she allowed herself to become pregnant because her religion
prevented her from using any contraceptive method?'
He stopped and pursed his lips. 'If she were that devout she wouldn't have had an affair in the first place.'

'Doesn't follow,' said Monica. 'Lots of Catholics
have affairs.'

'But they don't have babies.'

Another silence. 'I'll make some breakfast,' said Simon, erupting from the bed in sudden enthusiasm. 'Today will be a good day.' A few minutes later he
returned with a tray of coffee, Florida Orange and
toast.

'Maybe,' said Monica, 'she was trying to get the man
to marry her and the only way she could think of was
by threatening to have his baby.'

'It might have had the reverse effect.'

'Do you think the man was married?'

Bognor mused over the toast, which was charred.

'If it was someone on the column the only unmarried one is Viscount Wimbledon and he hasn't had time to get her three months pregnant. That leaves old Derby who is unlikely, Gringe, Port and Bertie Harris. Bertie Harris is inconceivable. As for the other two . . . I suppose "Sir" Milborn might have been having a "bit on the side" as he would undoubtedly put it. I suspect Granny Gringe is mercilessly henpecked and would like a shoulder to cry on but I doubt whether he has the ability or the enthusiasm to find one.'

He took away the breakfast and made more coffee. Then they dressed for a day in the country—Monica in a camel coloured trouser suit and a headscarf, he in a Donegal tweed jacket and pale corduroy trousers. He wondered about a tie but in the end wore a heavy roll neck sweater with a string vest underneath. It would be cold and he wanted to do some walking.

They were away soon after nine and Bognor drove down the new elevated Motorway which cut across Paddington, and then continued forty odd miles in the direction of Oxford before turning away from the main road and stopping to explore the area round Christmas Common. It was crisp but fine and they walked in silence for two hours, tramping across the spongey hillsides wet with the remains of the night's frost. Considering it was within an hour of the city the air felt clean and Bognor breathed deeply, almost gargling with it as if by doing so he could wash out the fumes of Fleet Street. Occasionally they would meet genuine ramblers—resolute figures with satchels and sticks and trousers tucked into knee-length stockings—but for the most part they were alone. Eventually Bognor tired of this rural heartiness. His stomach told him that it was, if not lunch time, at least time for a drink before lunch, and taking one last wistful look across the plain to Oxford in the distance he slapped his stomach, and said he'd like a pink gin. Or, if they could find one, a decent pint. Monica did not demur.

Quarter of an hour later they were sitting in the

lounge bar of a seventeenth-century pub called the Dragon's Tail which they had found on an empty lane, apparently equidistant between two villages. They were the only two in the bar except for the young barmaid and two earnest rambling ladies eating cheese and pickled onions in a far corner. Bognor bought two pints of bitter from the girl and sat down with Monica next to the log fire. She took a beer and handed him his clipboard.

'Cheers,' he said, getting froth up his nose. 'Now let's solve the murder.'

'Suspects,' he wrote at the top of the foolscap sheet. Then on the extreme left of the page he added one above the other but in no particular order: ' "Sir" Milborn Port, the Hon. Bertie Harris, Ms Molly Mortimer, E. Gringe Esq., and Viscount Wimbledon.' Then he had another swig of the beer which because it tasted woody and flat and was only just cold represented a good pint by his eclectic standards. 'As you see,' he said, 'the smart thing at the Pepys Show is to be a commoner. Titles are two a penny.'

'Now,' he said, 'the most interesting alibi for the first murder is Molly and Wimbledon's. They claim they were together in bed. So they have only each other and neither is trustworthy in my opinion. However, Molly can't have killed Anthea Morrison because she was with me. Therefore if the two murders are connected and Molly did the first then Wimbledon must have done the second.'

'I don't follow,' said Monica.

'No,' said Simon, scratching behind his ear with the pencil, 'nor do I. Now, listen. None of those people have real alibis for the Derby murder. Port could have come up quickly from Stoke Poges in his Jaguar, and all the others live within half an hour of the office. Even if their wives or lovers did notice they'd gone, they're not going to say so, are they?'

'No,' said Monica, 'but I don't understand why whoever it was wasn't spotted going into the *Globe* offices at that time of night. Derby was.'

'Because Derby went in the front and ordered a taxi and made very sure everyone knew he was there. I think he knew someone was going to try to knock him off. If that dozy doorman had got a taxi more quickly he might have prevented it. Remember the Chesterton lines:

> They cry in their parliament 'Who goes home?'
> And there comes no answer in arch or dome
> For none in the city of graves goes home.

He knew, Monica. If only he'd told that Parson Wood-forde character at the Harbingers' Dinner who it was he was going to meet.'

'Well he didn't,' said Monica flatly. 'Nice beer.'

'Not bad,' he said. 'No, whoever did it didn't want to be seen so he went in one of the back ways. That place is like a rabbit warren. If you know your way round you could wander in and out for days on end and no one would ever stop you. And at that time of night it's easier because the editorial people are mostly at home. If you worked as a reporter or writer the chances are you wouldn't be recognized even if you were seen.'

'So what are you saying?' asked Monica who was already half way through her pint. Bognor wondered if her liking for beer had anything to do with the way her bottom was beginning to droop.

'Nothing really, except that in a way Wharfedale's right. Ordinary police methods aren't going to apply in this. "Where were you at 11.15 on the night of . . .?" isn't going to solve it. It's got to be decided on motive and the more we scratch the more we find.' He scrawled motive alongside the word 'Suspects' and began at the top.

'Flogging filth to Russian intelligence', he wrote by Port's name, 'blackmailed by Derby. Fed up, unable to pay, etc. Confrontation.' He drank some more and watched the rich brown liquid disappearing. 'Milborn Port has the temper,' he said, 'even if it wasn't premeditated.'

He went and ordered two more pints and a couple of ploughman's lunches. 'Bertie Harris,' he said, when he was back by the fire, 'is a cool customer, but he may be a shade too cool. He said an odd thing to me and I think he was lying. He said that his father wanted to sack Derby but that the Union protected him. And the Imperial Father says that's not true. He might have misunderstood. Or the Union might be lying but I doubt it. Now why tell a lie like that?'

The lunches arrived and he chewed on a pickled onion. By Bertie Harris's name he wrote: 'Intends selling out to rival group when father dies. Derby found out. Blackmail. Confrontation as for Port.'

'Is that likely?' asked Monica. 'Wouldn't he be too cool to let something like that happen?'

'He's arrogant and self-satisfied. It's plausible enough.'

The two ramblers got up and left, shaking themselves down with an air of rugged superiority. They both smirked at Simon and Monica as they passed. "Smug pair,' he said. 'Little do they know that we've been striding seriously for two hours.'

'Not seriously by their standards,' said Monica. 'You're getting obese.'

'Nonsense,' he said as usual. 'I'm just big boned. Now what about Molly Mortimer?'

'She sounds just like a murderess,' said Monica with an edge to her voice, 'but then I expect most women journalists do.'

'Aha,' said Bognor. 'Jealous?'

'Not in the least,' said Monica reddening. 'She sounds like a poseur that's all.'

'You said she sounded like a murderess.'

'She does.'

'I don't think so. She's the only one of them who I don't think is blackmailable. She's appalling but she admits it. She doesn't care who knows what she gets up to. I'm going to cross her off the list.'

'Now I really am jealous.'

'Silly,' he squeezed Monica's thigh, which looked

chubby in the trouser suit and thought of Molly Mortimer in the housecoat with the cleavage. She was very desirable. He did hope he wasn't allowing his emotions to interfere with his judgement.

'I'll leave her on,' he said, 'just for you. But I can't think of a motive.'

Monica let out a little yelp of triumph and spluttered Cheddar over the table. 'I've got a smashing one,' she said. 'She rumbled Derby very early on, right?'

'Yes, when he tried to blackmail her lover, who was an M.P.'

'And then they made it up and he took her out to lunch and they became all buddy-buddy.'

'What a vile expression.'

She was unabashed. 'Your friend Molly Mortimer tried to blackmail him back. That's what she did. And then they compromised and decided to make it a partnership. Finally she got too greedy. Probably asked for more than her 50 per cent. *And* now that she's in love with the little Viscount she's decided to go into partnership with him. She got him to kill the Morrison girl because she knew too much.'

'That's ridiculous.' Bognor spread some butter on the crusty home-made bread and frowned. 'I'm sure it wasn't a woman who killed him. A woman wouldn't have the strength. Besides she was the one who first put me on to the idea of Derby's blackmail game.'

'There you are then,' said Monica, excitedly, 'game, set and match. What better way to divert attention. Classic ploy. And as for not being strong enough to stab him, first I don't believe it, and secondly she probably didn't do her own dirty work. She got the wretched Wimbledon to do it and provided him with an alibi at the same time. She's Lady Macbeth I tell you. And for that,' she said, draining her second pint and wiping her lips with the back of her hand, 'I'll have another pint.'

'You'll make yourself fat,' he said grudgingly. 'It's quite clever I grant you that, but it's pretty unlikely.'

'Balls,' she said, 'and if you won't get me one I'll get one myself.'

Bognor shrugged and watched her march to the bar and order two pints and more pickled onions. An old mongrel staggered in from behind the bar and lay down in front of the fire. Bognor was reminded inconsequentially of the adage about teaching an old dog new tricks. It wasn't a bad theory.

'What about Granny Gringe?' he said. 'He's next on the list.'

'I thought I'd solved it for you,' she said, 'but if you insist we'll finish your bloody list. From what you said I should suggest he's far too wet. If you don't think Molly Mortimer had the strength and the guts I can't for the life of me understand how you think Gringe could have done it. And why anyway?'

'Blackmail, like the others?'

'Why?'

'Perhaps he was the one who got Anthea Morrison pregnant. He looks like a man who needs an affair and he had a lot in common with her. They were the only two in the office who were constantly ignored or patronized.'

'And if he was having an affair? That's hardly blackmailable these days?'

'I bet it is in Bromley,' said Bognor, 'but even if it isn't Lord Wharfedale wouldn't approve. He's a puritan zealot and apart from that sleeping with secretaries is considered bad form. They'd have had him out for that.'

'But you don't even know that he was sleeping with the secretary,' protested Monica.

'Any more than you know that Molly Mortimer formed a blackmailing alliance with St John Derby.'

'No but . . .'

'No buts. There's one left—Willy Wimbledon.'

'We've done him. He's in league with Miss Mortimer.'

'Why?'

'Because he's infatuated with her. I told you it's

Macbeth. The poor lad doesn't know what he's doing.'

Bognor sucked his teeth again, and realized he'd got a piece of pickled onion stuck in them. 'Not convinced,' he said, trying to extricate the bit of onion. 'I'm not sure about his sexual preferences, despite his protestations, and I think he knows very well what he's doing. There are fewer flies on Viscount Wimbledon than most people imagine.'

They both stared into their beer and were interrupted by the barmaid. 'I'm afraid it's closing time,' she said, 'I don't want to rush you, but we could lose our licence, so if you wouldn't mind drinking up.'

They drank up. Bognor felt replete and drowsy. Outside he made use of the evil-smelling gentlemen's lavatory and stood by the car waiting for Monica to emerge from the ladies'.

'Well,' she said, giving him a neat peck on the cheek, 'have we solved it?'

'No,' said Bognor, 'we've just made it worse.' And they turned their backs on the declining sun and drove east towards the scene of the crimes.

It was grey and darkening when they reached home. Bognor still felt sleepy and he was irritated. He had wanted to look at Derby's old flat while it was still light. It was too bad. He supposed that he could do it in the morning on the way to the Seven-a-side tournament at Rosslyn Park's ground in the South West of London but something made him want to get it over with. The keys were waiting on the doormat in a brown manila envelope. Inside there was a brief note from Sanders: 'Be careful. See you Monday.'

'I think I'll go and peer round now,' he said to Monica, 'do you want to come? I'd be less conspicuous on my own.' Monica said she'd stay and have a bath, reminded him that they were due at the Kirkbrides for drinks at seven and made him promise to be back soon. It wouldn't be difficult. Twenty minutes to Kensington. Twenty minutes to snoop and then twenty minutes to get back again. He promised to be back by six at the very latest.

The Derby residence was the top floor of a large early Victorian mansion close to the South Kensington underground station—three minutes walk it had been at St John Derby's ambling gait though it was no more than a hundred yards away. The front door was open and gave the appearance, unusual in this area, of being permanently so. Bognor took in the expensive carpet, the bell marked 'Caretaker' and decided to use the stairs rather than the lift. He went up them slowly, because he was unfit, and carefully because he had been warned. At the top he paused briefly in front of the cream door and noticed that there was a peep hole cut in the middle of it. A reasonable enough precaution.

He put the key in the lock and was about to turn it when he saw some rough chip marks round it that looked almost as if they might have been made by a chisel. That was peculiar. The door had been forced. It must, he supposed, have been the police, though why they should have bothered to do that when they already had a set of keys he couldn't imagine. He mentally echoed Lord Wharfedale's opinion of them as clodhopping oafs and let himself in.

The hall was long and gloomy with three gilt wall brackets, each one holding two electric lights in the shape of candles. They were to Bognor's eyes cheap and inelegant but that was not what struck him as odd. They were on.

He stiffened momentarily, just inside the door. The police or the caretaker must have left them burning. It was careless. Criminal indeed with the current state of the nation and the Energy Minister demanding economies in the home. He listened, still suspicious, but he could hear nothing. For a moment he thought of turning them off but then grinned and marched decisively up the carpet to the door at the end. There were others leading off the hall but the one at the end looked the most important and so indeed it was.

It was dark inside but he could clearly see the view from the huge picture window at the far end of the room. It gave out onto the square which was half lit and like the house itself sturdy, sensible and very British. There was also a large garden, shared, he guessed, with the other residents. He stood for a moment staring down into it and then walked back to the door and turned on the switch, which operated an enormous cut glass chandelier hanging from a massive lavatory-like chain in the centre of the ceiling. It was an impressive room by any standards, very impressive indeed by the standards which, he judged, were maintained by most Fleet Street journalists. He couldn't imagine that chez Gringe in Bromley was in quite the same league and even Molly Mortimer's, which by his admittedly frugal standards could almost be labelled sumptuous was mean by comparison. One long wall was taken up entirely with books, many of which looked like collectors' items. He picked one out at random and saw that it was a first edition of Mungo Park's diaries.

The stereo, which Molly had mentioned with some awe, and the colour television were both built into highly polished mahogany cabinets; the fireplace was huge and marble and over it hung the Augustus John, which had an unfinished air about it, and was of a young man with curiously fleshy lips. The carpet was almost as deep as Lord Wharfedale's and on it were two rugs which Bognor, who knew nothing about it, judged to be Persian.

He gazed round admiring the deep sofas upholstered in leather and velvet, deploring an eighteenth-century Chinoiserie backgammon table and a bad oil painting of a naked boy running through what looked like a field of giant buttercups. It was difficult to know quite what he was searching for but the place certainly conveyed atmosphere. He could almost imagine the old boy lurching in with his cloak billowing out behind him. He was just visualizing this unlikely apparition when he suddenly felt a twinge of apprehension in the pit of his stomach. It unnerved him because it was the unromantic queasy feeling he usually experienced when he was terrified out of his wits. And he usually only felt it when he had good reason to be scared. A second later he knew that his feeling hadn't let him down. Someone was padding softly down the hall. Away from him. The thickly piled carpet almost obliterated the sound but then he heard the door squeak as it was opened. He had been rooted to the large Persian rug for a full five seconds but as he heard the door he suddenly became galvanized and ran out in the direction of the noise. The door was slamming shut just as he arrived in the hall. He raced up the carpet and reached the far end in time to hear the unmistakeable scrape of a key being turned against him. He felt quickly in his jacket pocket and then groaned with dismay. Idiot, he said to himself, out loud. He had been so preoccupied with the lights in the hall that he had forgotten to take his key out of the door. It was *his* key which was turning now on the outside. Locking him in. He froze in an agony of recrimination and fury, not unmixed with dread. As he stood he could hear footsteps walking slowly away towards the stairs, then they faded as, presumably, they reached them and finally became silent.

'Oh God' he said very loudly, and stamped petulantly three times. He could kill himself. For a few moments he stayed there swearing uncontrollably. Then he laughed. It was difficult to see the funny side of his predicament but he felt sure there was one. Optimistically he peered through the keyhole and saw light. The key had been removed. He walked back down the hall and wondered what to do next. In the drawing room he sprawled on the most comfortable sofa and gazed blankly at the gilt coffee table in front of him. It had a Victorian glass paperweight on it, also the latest copies of *Playgirl, The Connoisseur* and The Wine Society's Report. By them was a silver ash tray on a swivel above a little bucket which he recognized as being designed by Arne Jacobson. To the right of that was a copy of *Wisden* in its distinctive yellow cloth binding. He picked it up and saw that it was the volume for

1938. That was the year, he remembered, that Hutton made 364 in the Oval Test Match out of a total of 903. He prided himself on his knowledge of cricketing statistics. England had been playing the Australians and the next most prolific batsman had been Maurice Leyland with a hundred and sixty something. He couldn't remember the exact score and after a moment's guessing settled on 164 before opening the book to discover if he was right.

As he opened it he swore again. 'Those bloody fool police,' he said. 'That idiot Sanders.'

The *Wisden* was a fat volume and the first fifty and the last fifty pages were intact. The intervening hundreds, however, had been interfered with. The entire middle section of the book had been cut away, leaving a rectangular hole the size of a cigarette packet. 'St John Derby's safe,' he said softly. 'The clever old bastard.' He glanced up at the bookshelves and saw that the *Wisdens* were at the very top, well away from the casually prying eye. Immediately underneath was a small step ladder, put there, he guessed, by the mysterious interloper. He climbed it himself and took out the 1937 copy. It was unspoilt, virgin, not a page nor a line missing. He replaced it and tried 1936 which was similarly intact, and continued to 1929 with equal lack of success. 1928 however was in the same state as 1938. There was, needless to say, nothing in the hiding place. He tried 1948, 1958 and 1968 and it was the same. Each one had its hole in the middle, and not one had anything in that hole. Whoever had been there that afternoon had got the lot. At least that was what Bognor assumed. One of St John Derby's victims had forced his way in and stolen all the incriminating evidence the diarist had possessed. He guessed there was enough space in the almanacks to contain the ruin of dozens of reputations. Hundreds if he'd used microfilm. Bognor put each book back in its place and returned to the sofa. His problem now was to escape.

The picture window was his first thought but another glimpse of the view quickly dissuaded him. He was about four floors up, he had no head for heights and the drainpipes looked precarious. A swift shufti round the flat showed that there were no other doors. By the time he'd established that he was genuinely trapped it was after six. Monica would soon start to worry. He sat down on the sofa again and supposed he'd better tell her what had happened. There was a vintage black telephone half hidden behind a yellowing fern in the hall and to Bognor's irrational surprise it worked. He dialed her number.

'Thank God,' she said. 'What's happened? Where are you?'

Briefly and shamefacedly Bognor explained.

'You'd better get the fire brigade,' she said brightly. Now that she realized he was relatively safe and the victim only of his own carelessness she sounded peeved.

'Don't be ridiculous,' he said. 'I'm not supposed to be here.'

'I know,' she sighed, 'but you *are* there and you might as well get used to the idea. What am I supposed to do anyway? Go to the Kirkbrides on my own? Tell them you're indisposed? Isn't there a caretaker or someone you can telephone?'

Bognor stifled an expletive and blushed. It must be the beer, he decided. Or the shock. There were some phone books on the shelves underneath the table. 'I'll be with you soon,' he said, 'I'll think of something.'

It was simple. He found the address of the block in the phone book, telephoned and the caretaker downstairs answered.

'I'm terribly sorry to trouble you,' he said, 'I'm the nephew of the late St John Derby and I've just been going through one or two of his things and now I find I've very foolishly locked myself in. I wonder if you could be good enough to come up and let me out?'

The caretaker didn't sound any too bright. 'Nephew, eh? Locked in, are you? I'll be with you in a jiffy. I'm just having my tea.'

Bognor sauntered back to the drawing room and sat

down to wait. The minutes ticked by. Five. Ten. The bloody man, he thought and conjured up a vision of a surly servant in baggy trousers and a vest, malingering over baked beans and a mug of tea. Monica was going to be livid. Another five minutes passed. From down below in the street he heard a siren from a police car or ambulance. He wondered if he should telephone again and began to pace restlessly round the room. Then to his relief he heard voices beyond the door, the scrabbling of keys and, in an instant, heavy footsteps pounded down the hall. Several of them, in pairs. And when they came into the drawing room he saw to his consternation that he had some explaining to do. It was the police, in large quantities.

They arrived at the Kirkbrides eventually. They were the last, of course. But dinner had barely started. He had explained to the police, who had eventually and grudgingly sent for Sanders. Sanders had explained to him, roughly and gracelessly, that they had been half expecting something of the sort and that the caretaker had been briefed to report any stranger heading for Derby's flat. Bognor, tactlessly, for by then he had been very angry, had upbraided the caretaker for not noticing the real intruder and the police for not discovering the secret hiding places in the *Wisden Cricketers' Almanacks*. There had been an ugly row. The words 'amateur', 'buffoon', 'incompetent' and 'bungler' had been freely bandied and there had been oaths. They had not parted on friendly terms.

On his return to the flat he had attempted further explanations but Monica had been no more receptive than the boorish Sanders. She used many of the same words as Sanders and there were more oaths. But eventually they arrived at the Kirkbrides, where they had a vile dinner and Bognor was bored rigid.

7

Bognor began the next day with the boundless optimism of a man who has known so many recent disappointments that, on the law of averages, they must come to an end. Unfortunately in Bognor's case the law of averages did not apply. At the beginning of the day however he was in high spirits. As he drove over Hammersmith Bridge the sunlight caught the waters of the Thames which sparkled back merrily. The tide was high and oarsmen in singlets skiffed about in improbable vessels. Church bells tolled for morning service and Bognor sang. His mouth was very much less painful today and the words were easier to pronounce and, better still, easier for others to understand. He sang flat but he sang happily:

> Olim fuit monachorum
> Schola nostra sedes
> Puer regius illorum
> Fecit nos heredes.

Once upon a time he had known what the words meant but he had long since forgotten. The words themselves had stayed embedded in his subconscious. It was hardly surprising since they'd been beaten into it by prefects at school.

> Hoc in posteros amoris
> Grande dedit signum
> Sonet ergo fundatoris
> Nomen laude dignum.

Then came the chorus, much more easily memorable and rather silly, 'Vivat Rex Eduardus Sextus, Vivat Vivat Vivat, Vivat Rex Eduardus Sextus, Vivat Vivat Vivat.' His car was drawn up at traffic lights by the

Red Lion pub when he noticed the driver of the next car looking at him peculiarly. Bognor realized that his discordant singing had been extremely boisterous. He wound the window up and felt hurt. The first shadow across his cloudless day.

At Rosslyn Park he realized why he had regurgitated the words of the old school song. The place hadn't changed since the days when he and his schoolfriends had chanted it on the touchline during the national schools' seven-a-side competition and for adults the setting was evidently similar. The people, for instance, were identical. In the old days he had assumed that they were parents but now he saw that they were just rugby fans. Men with gumboots and cloth caps pulled down over their foreheads, woollen scarves and briar pipes stuck permanently in the corners of their mouths. Women with shooting sticks and harsh voices and a tendency to shout upsettingly violent advice during games: 'Tackle him *low*, Lorimer', 'Use your *feet*, Anstruther' or in moment of severe anguish 'Screw him, Lorimer' or 'Knock him *over*, Anstruther'. Once when Bognor had been playing he had heard someone scream 'Have his balls off, Bognor' and was certain it had been a female voice. It had been embarrassing.

The cars parked in erratic lines tended to be old rusty Rovers or spanking new Volvo Estate cars but it was down by the main pitch with its dingy corrugated iron stand and its functional brick pavilion and its old men selling programmes that Bognor noticed the most evocative reminder of his youth and the most profound difference. The first was the beer tent behind the goal posts at the far end, a dingy grey marquee through whose portals he could see barrels on trestles and men in duffle coats, elbows purposefully bent as they put back the first pints of the morning. The second were the posters. All over the place: 'The *Daily Globe* Rugby Sevens', 'The Truth, the Whole Truth and Nothing but the Truth', 'The Samuel Pepys Column— the truth about people—is here', 'Rex Shuttle, the *Globe* trotting man of Sport is here', 'Give the *Globe* a

Sporting Chance—Read it now'. And so on. Bognor frowned. It was supposed to be an amateur game. This sort of thing was all very well but . . .

He wondered where the press tent was. It had been agreed that they would convene there before being allocated specific tasks. He wondered if Milborn Port would have recovered his temper enough to put in an appearance and whether Eric Gringe was well enough to come. There should be no problem with any of the others, though he wondered what Viscount Wimbledon was going to write. 'I score the winning points in tearjerking cliffhanger', he supposed. Musing thus, he almost bumped into the Viscount.

'I say, hello,' he said. 'Are you going to the press tent? It's round the back of the beer tent. They're all there. I'm just going to warm up.'

Bognor looked at the blond tracksuited figure and frowned more. The young peer looked revolting athletic. The track suit was pale blue with a white trim and at his neck he wore a silk scarf nonchalantly knotted. He didn't look to Bognor like a man who was going to get his knees dirty.

'Thanks,' he said, 'I'll go and find them. And good luck.'

'Thank you,' he smiled boyishly, 'I'll need it.'

Bognor turned and shuffled off towards the beer tent, his spirits momentarily dampened by the apparition of glorious youth which conjured up visions of his lost past. Not, to be honest that Bognor had ever looked anything but overweight and middle-aged. Nevertheless ten years ago when he was the Viscount's age he had looked *less* overweight and middle-aged.

There was a profusion of bunting around the beer tent. Seedy much used bunting, it still gave a touch of gaiety. Bognor pushed back his shoulders and pulled in his stomach and then decided to pick up a pint on his way to the official tent. He stepped gingerly across some guy ropes, past a gaggle of schoolmaster types in striped scarves and almost upset the frothing pint which 'Sir' Milborn Port was raising with an unsteady hand.

'Ah,' said Mr Port nervously, 'I thought I ought to have a word with you. I've been putting two and two together. Have a drink.'

Bognor saw that he was drinking neat whisky and washing it down with beer. He looked dreadful. His face was puce and puffy and his eyes rheumy. His outfit was more suited to a day's racing than a day's rugby but not of a distinguished sort. He wore a belted brown overcoat, a bedraggled brown trilby and from his neck there hung a battered binocular case festooned with the tickets of innumerable racecourses rather as extrovert travellers cover their baggage with airline stickers. From the folds of his voluminous overcoat there protruded a pair of cavalry twill encased legs and two down at heel suede desert boots which had recently been through a puddle.

'I'd like a pint.'

The pint came and Milborn gave it to him and put a hand on his shoulder.

'Mind if we go over there for a chat?' He winked as he said it and nodded in the direction of a table in a corner where the tent canvas flapped in the wind.

'OK.'

At the table Milborn put down his glasses and extracted a packet of cheroots and a packet of mints from the folds of his greatcoat. Bognor took a cigar but declined the mint and eventually with much difficulty caused by the trembling of his hands and the draughts coming through holes in the canvas Milborn managed to ignite the cigars.

'You're on to me, aren't you?' he said, leaning across the table and coughing out cigar smoke, 'I'm rumbled.'

Bognor wondered what he was talking about. It was clear he wasn't well and he was rambling. He leant even farther across the table and Bognor recoiled involuntarily from the stench of mints and alcohol and tobacco and simple primitive halitosis. 'Come on,' he said, 'honour between thieves. I know your game.'

'What game?' said Bognor. He didn't like the way

this conversation was developing. He looked about the tent anxiously for help but the faces were universally strange.

'You know, don't you?' Mr Port tried to tap his finger against his nose and missed, waving thin air pathetically. He tried again and managed more successfully.

'Know what?' Bognor imagined he was talking about his grubby liaison with the Russian Embassy.

'Vodka,' he said, as if it was a password, 'Ivan the terrible, blinis.'

Bognor realized that he was doing an impression of the Spy Who Came In From The Cold. He decided to humour him.

'You mean I know that you have, shall we say, *dealings* with Russian intelligence.'

'Not so loud,' hissed Mr Port, looking furtively at the flapping canvas and the knots of stolid rugby enthusiasts. 'You have to be careful in this line of country.'

'Of course,' said Bognor, 'Silly of me.'

'I suppose,' Milborn took a swig of whiskey and then filled his mouth with beer before swallowing both together, 'you think I've sold out.'

'The thought had crossed my mind.'

Milborn shook his head vehemently, and dropped his voice almost to the point of inaudibility. 'That's what they want you to think,' he said ambiguously. 'I give them a lot of duff information. I'm more what you'd call a double-agent.'

'Oh I see,' said Bognor gently. 'In that case it doesn't matter. I mean I'll keep quiet.'

'You'd better do that. Hardly anyone knows and if anyone found out it could be very dangerous.'

'Ah.' The only thing that impressed Bognor was that Milborn appeared to have rumbled his true identity. He doubted whether it was a piece of individual detection. Much more likely to have been a tip from his friends at the Embassy. In which case he was definitely rather flattered. It meant he was acquiring a reputation.

'Now,' Milborn was jabbing his finger about and

speaking very slowly, 'I think this St John business is a deliberate attempt to frame me. They're trying to get me out of the way.'

'They?'

The secret agent looked self-consciously secretive and jerked his eyes heavenwards.

'Oh I see,' said Bognor, not seeing anything but sensing that he should continue to humour him. 'Was St John blackmailing you?'

For a moment a yellow look of animal cunning flashed across the drunken face. 'He thought he was,' he said. 'I used to pay him a bit to keep his mouth shut. Otherwise he'd have given the whole game away.'

It sounded to Bognor like an accurate description of blackmail but he didn't say so. There didn't seem any point. 'So,' he asked, 'who do you think killed him?'

The papal claimant shrugged expressively. 'I don't suppose,' he said, portentously, 'that we'll ever know.'

Silly old soak, thought Bognor, and found his private thoughts being echoed out loud.

'Silly old soaks,' said Molly Mortimer, 'I said you'd be in here. Come on, for Christ's sake, before Granny has a coronary.'

Miss Mortimer was dressed entirely in fur—fur boots, fur coat almost to her ankles and a fur hood. Very little of her was showing, but what was smiled indulgently at Bognor. He wondered if Monica could have been right. She'd make an exquisite blackmailer. Could it have been her in the flat yesterday? Perhaps Milborn Port had been right in his maddening way. Perhaps he would never know anything.

Molly put a furry arm through his and suggested they walk along the duckboards which had been arranged like stepping stones to keep the elegantly shod out of the grass and dirt.

'There's an atmosphere,' she said. 'No one has been forgiven for anything and everyone is mysteriously to blame for everything. Your bruises have gone down. Willy promises he'll buy you a drink when the games are over. He really is sorry.'

'Hmm. I saw him. He looked rather pleased with himself.'

'Don't be beastly. I said I'd make it up to you.' She gave Bognor a conspiratorially sexy look and marched into the press tent with a swagger.

The headquarters of the Samuel Pepys column for the day was one end of a plain trestle table. At the other end were specialist sports writers and a news reporter. Granny Gringe sat at his end with the temporary secretary whose skirt had ridden even higher exposing fleshy goosepimpled thigh under the stockings. He seemed distraught, twitching in all directions and with discoloured purple disfiguring his otherwise pallid complexion.

'Ah *there* you are, Bognor. I want you to cover the outside pitches before lunch, with Molly. They're up by the golf course. Plenty of zip and colour and keep an eye open for anecdotes and celebrities. Most of the celebrities will be round the main pitch this afternoon but a few may, er, sneak in this morning. And if we can have some copy at lunch that will help.'

There were typewriters on the table. The same antiques that featured so prominently in the *Globe* offices. Gringe had a telephone too, a primitive object connected to the world outside the tent by a thick cable.

The rest of the world's press had a single table and two telephones between the lot of them. It was well known in Fleet Street that while dog didn't eat dog, dog didn't scratch other dog's back either. Therefore whenever one newspaper sponsored an event they made sure that their rivals were accommodated in the most inferior manner possible. Each newspaper at the table had a stiff wooden chair to itself and a cardboard sign in front giving the name. Bognor saw that the only other journalist present was an elderly gentleman sitting in the space reserved for the Press Association. A zipper bag lay at his feet and on the table in front of him there was a tartan thermos flask and a packet of sandwices. He was reading a paperback.

'They kick off in five minutes, so look sharp,' said

Gringe, 'and please someone try to produce a usable
item. Remember, Bognor, Lord Wharfedale's words.
Flair. I should appreciate some flair today if it's possible. More flair and less drinking in bars with Mr Port.
But above all, please some copy.'

'I'll try,' he said. He had no idea what he was going
to write about.

Up by the golf course the teams were already lining
up. There were two pitches, both improvised for the
occasion and therefore sloping and rutted in a way
which introduced an unusual element of chance into the
proceedings. Bognor, to his pleasure, recognized the
distinctive magenta and gold hoops of the Terrapins on
the pitch nearest him. He decided to watch the performance of Viscount Wimbledon, while Molly, reluctantly,
wandered to the ground next door where a team called
the Druids were engaged with one called the Bosuns.

The wind was blowing fiercely from the north, tear-
ing at the corner flags and the spectators' caps and
making it difficult to kick the ball with any degree of
accuracy or even to catch it. It would be interesting to
see how young Willy performed. The game was tailor
made for someone like him with, Bognor guessed, a
turn of speed and a lot of dexterity. As it only lasted a
quarter of an hour sheer rugged stamina was not important, and sheer brute strength which was vital in the
full sized fifteen-a-side game which lasted an hour and
a half, was almost an impediment. This was a game
for the fleet of foot and the Terrapins looked just that.
Beside their opponents, a gang of burly flatfoots from
Cornwall, they looked distinctly flimsy but Bognor
guessed they would have little difficulty in demolishing
them.

The referee, a dapper figure in green, blew his
whistle and the Cornish kicked off into the wind. The
egg shaped leather hovered in the air and gyrated in
the wind as it descended. The Cornish charged after it,
elbows swinging and heads down. Bognor saw that the
man underneath the descending ball was Willy Wim-

bledon. He caught it clearly and with a neat jink
evaded the leading Cornishman and ran swiftly upfield. Just as a second opponent seemed on the point of
flattening him the Viscount hurled the ball to a team-
mate standing ten yards from him. This, Bognor
sensed, was the Terrapins' 'flyer' and so it turned out.
With a devastating sprint the man hurtled successfully
over the Cornish goal line and dropped the ball for a
try. Four points to nil. There was an outbreak of clapping from the few hundred spectators and some shouts
of 'Played Terrapins', 'Good run, Bagley', and one
from a distinguished fifty-year-old man on a shooting
stick near Bognor. 'Well out, Willy,' he called approv-
ingly. It was an intelligent piece of approbation. The
Terrapin sprinter had scored the try but it was Wimbledon who had made it possible with the neat catch,
the clever sidestep and the beautifully timed pass. It
was Wimbledon who took the conversion kick. Effort-
lessly he nudged it between the uprights and over the
bar. Two more points, more clapping, a shout of
'Kicked, Willy', from the man on the shooting stick.
The Viscount ran back to join his team-mates with a
modest wave of acknowledgement. Bognor found himself disliking him intensely.

The rest of the game was sadly one-sided. The Terrapins' tactics were simple. With some dexterity,
mainly from Willy, they manoeuvred the ball to Bagley
on the wing who was several yards faster than any
Cornishman and cantered over for tries with relentless
regularity.

Wimbledon then kicked the conversions with decep-
tive ease. Bognor knew that in the gale force wind it
was a difficult task. Eventually the Terrapins scored
thirty-six points. The Cornish scored only once in a
manner which he found significant. Willy had kicked
off and the ball was caught by the Goliath of the Cornish side. Scorning refinement this bulldozer of a man
put his head down and charged straight at the Viscount. He presented a terrifying spectacle and for a
moment it seemed as if Willy would be trampled under

foot, but it was not to be. In an instant he had blundered past leaving Willy spreadeagled but apparently undamaged. Despite his lack of pace he still outstripped his pursuers, of whom Willy was not one, and scored under the post.

'Bad luck, Willy,' shouted Bognor's neighbour on the stick. 'Bugger the bad luck,' muttered Bognor under his breath. It had been clear cowardice. The man on the shooting stick was either pig ignorant or hoplelssly biased. Bognor looked across at him as the final whistle blew and thought he detected a family resemblance. Of course. The Early of Surrey. Willy's father. Bognor wondered if he counted as a celebrity and decided that he came within the meaning of the act. Pulling out his notebook he decided to attempt an interview.

'Er . . . excuse me.'

'Yes.' Not unfriendly. Just surprised. Bognor was surprised he hadn't seen the resemblance earlier. The father was the spitting image of the son, thirty years on, with precisely the same slightly effeminate good looks, only gone a little to seed.

'I'm from the Samuel Pepys column. Simon Bognor. Could I have a word?'

'Of course. Didn't Willy have a good game?'

'Very. Did you play yourself . . . sir.' He didn't see why he should call the Earl 'sir' but felt that Granny Gringe would have required it.

'No. It's quite a new departure at Eton.'

They talked mundanely for a few minutes before Bognor thanked him and wandered off to find Molly and watch the second game, which had just begun. He had enough for a dull paragraph.

'God I hate this,' said Molly, stamping her feet. 'I wish I was at home and in bed. By the way I've told them about you. I hope you don't mind.'

Bognor stamped with her. It was odd how cold it could be with the sun still shining. 'How do you mean, told them?'

'About the *Winnipeg Eagle* and the Board of Trade. It seemed so silly not to.'

Bognor thought for a moment. 'You knew already,' he said, 'because I told you. Willy knew because you explained to him after you say he hit me. Bertie Harris knew because his father told him. And I think someone else told Milborn. So the only person who hasn't been formally told is Eric Gringe. And if he hadn't guessed already he's sillier than I thought.'

'He's sillier than you thought then,' said Molly. 'He was the only one who seemed at all surprised. I was quite put out.'

The game in front of them was a more two-sided affair than the Terrapins versus the Cornish but much less speedy. They paid as little attention to it as possible.

'Have you been to St John Derby's flat?' he asked her suddenly.

She seemed unperturbed. 'Not for years. He had us all to a party about five years ago and before that I hadn't seen it since we had that mad passionate fling I was telling you about. Why do you ask?'

'I was wondering if you knew anything about the *Wisdens*?'

She looked at him evenly. '*Wisdens?*'

'*Wisden Cricketers' Almanack.* Bound in bright yellow. He had a full set.'

'What a funny question. I'm not very interested in cricket. It's quite pretty looking but I don't understand it. Still the weather's usually better than this.'

'But you don't remember the books?'

'Bound in yellow? . . . Now you mention it, yes, perhaps I do vaguely. Weren't they up at the top of that mammoth case?'

'Yes.'

'Well? What about them?'

'Oh . . . nothing.' Bognor suddenly felt despairing. 'Have you got any stories?' he asked. 'I've had a chat with Wimbledon's father, but nothing else.'

'No,' she said, 'but it doesn't matter. Let's go and have a quick drink.'

*   *   *

There was another drink tent nearer than the large beer marquee, and from it they could see across the main pitch. This time they had brandy and stood in the entrance watching seven men from Cumberland laying into another seven from Hertfordshire. On the other side of the pitch Bognor noticed a small motorized caravan whose roof had been turned into an improvised grandstand or viewing platform. A balustrade surrounded it and half a dozen people with glasses and binoculars were standing on it putting on a brave show of taking an interest.

'That's the brass,' said Molly. 'Wharfedale and the editors and some of the board. Bertie will appear up there before long. He doesn't really enjoy slumming with the rest of us.'

Bognor peered. He could see Wharfedale standing at the front of the group, a bowlegged figure in a strange stetson-like hat and a brown coat with velvet reveres. He seemed engrossed.

'What are we going to write about?' asked Bognor again.

'Why not do the Plynlimmon Wanderers' Goat?' said Molly. 'We haven't done it for a couple of years and Wharfedale's fond of it.'

The Plynlimmon Wanderers' Goat turned out to be the mascot of a team of Welsh slate miners. Bognor found it cropping grass quietly behind the pavilion. He spent some time walking round it and then chatted to the pretty girl who was supervising it. She turned out to be the captain's fiancée so he included her in his story about the goat. Then he bumped into Freddie ffrench-Patrick who he'd known vaguely at school and who had gone on to captain England and the British Lions and achieved nationwide fame as the scorer of ffrench-Patrick's try—the winning score in a historic encounter with the New Zealand All Blacks. He had run seventy-five yards to make it and was later found to have been suffering from a dislocated shoulder. Bognor discovered that he was now a stockbroker. He wrote it all down in his notebook and began to regain confidence and optimism. Three stories done. His watch said half past twelve. One more before lunch and he would be a popular diarist.

At one corner of the main pitch there was a large notice board on an easel which gave up-to-the-minute details of the competition's progress. In the early rounds the teams were divided into a series of leagues designed to eliminate all but eight. From that moment on the tournament became a straightforward knock-out with quarter-finals, semi-finals, a play-off between the losing semi-finalists to determine the third place and finally, just as it was beginning to get dark, the grand final itself for the Globe Trophy, an immense challenge cup in the shape of a rugger ball. Solid South African gold.

He paused by the board and saw that the Terrapins had completed their morning's programme with an unbeaten record. No doubt Willy Wimbledon had been impressing all and sundry.

'Got plenty of useful copy I hope?' It was Granny Gringe. He was hatless and wore a beige raincoat and galoshes. It was painfully obvious that he was not enjoying himself.

'I think three,' said Bognor and told him.

'I'm glad about the goat,' he said. 'Lord Warfedale's very attached to that goat. Dai isn't it?'

'No. Dai died two years ago. This is his son Taffy.'

'Ah.' Eric Gringe seemed abstracted. He took out a notebook and wrote down Bognor's three ideas. 'It sounds as if Willy's doing well.'

'Yes,' Bognor knew he sounded grudging. 'I'm surprised. He doesn't look rugged enough to excel at this.'

Gringe smiled tightly. 'I think you'll find Master Wimbledon will do very well at anything if he things it will forward his career. He's an exceedingly ruthless and ambitious young man. Very dangerous under certain circumstances.' There was a wavering note of underlying hysteria in his voice which Bognor found disconcerting. 'By the way,' he went on. 'I must talk to you. Later. Molly tells me that . . . well . . . that you're not really an ordinary journalist.'

'I thought you'd have guessed.'

'I prefer to know as little as possible about what goes on around me,' he said, hunching his shoulders. 'The more I learn the less I like it. We're all rogues and charlatans it seems.'

'You look as if you need a holiday,' said Bognor, not unkindly.

'I take very little holiday. They find it very hard to run the column when I'm away. And now that St John . . .' He smiled weakly and Bognor had a terrible feeling that he was going to break down there and then. He took the coward's way out.

'I'll just run and see if I can't dredge up another story before lunch,' he said breezily and hurried off in the direction of the golf course. He found one luckily. A team called the Seven Sisters' Stompers which had been losing by increasingly embarrassing margins turned out to be a jazz band which had entered as a joke, never having played the game before. Bognor dutifully wrote it all down and thought about murders.

He typed out his stories over a pint of beer and then joined the others in the drink tent where stale sandwiches and pork pies were provided. They were all there except for Willy who was doubtless lunching off steak and fresh orange juice to keep his strength up. It was an oddly tense gathering. Bognor had supposed that the neuroses and depressions of the diarists would diminish after the deaths. Being callous cynics they should have adjusted quickly after the initial shocks but instead they got worse. It could be, he thought, that it was purely selfish—that they were all scared of being accused. Also there were so many skeletons in so many cupboards that even if they weren't afraid of being done for murder they could be apprehensive about some other piece of dirty washing being hung out by Bognor or the police.

Nobody talked much. Milborn Port was too plastered to manage anything coherent. Every time he began a sentence you could see him working out the words beforehand, avoiding any long ones that he might stumble over and getting his mouth into position for careful and terribly precise enunciation. Eric Gringe was twitching furiously. Bertie Harris seemed detached and censorious. In any case he left after a cheese and chutney sandwich in order to have a brandy with his father and the top brass. Molly made a few brittle attempts at jollity but they fell sadly flat. He himself was ruminating about the murders. He only had three days after today before Lord Wharfedale would demand a result, and he didn't know that he was going to be able to do it. He had a nasty feeling that he was going to have to initiate some action. No one else was going to make a move so he would have to do some smoking out himself. He was, he knew, desperately short of real evidence, but there was one tiny bit which didn't fit, and increasingly he was inclined to chance everything on that. He frowned. It would be a hell of a risk and if it didn't work . . .

That afternoon all play took place on the main pitch. Hearty red-faced men began to arrive in droves and the crowds round the beer tents and bars swelled. The temporary urinals, little more than corrugated iron drainpipes behind canvas screens, attracted such custom that a short and permanent queue formed outside. By the time the Terrapins took the field for their quarter final against the Visigoths there were a few thousand spectators and despite the chill wind there was a promising air of carnival. The Visigoths were a stronger team than anything the Terrapins had met before but they nevertheless scraped through, Wimbledon again well to the fore. He looked undeniably glamorous in his magenta and gold, long blond hair flying out behind him. His shorts and knees were still remarkably clean Bognor noticed and a little knot of teeny bopper girls had fallen into noisy love with him, setting up a shrill chant of 'We want Willy' every time he got the ball. Bognor continued to wander about looking rather aimlessly for 'colour'. On one occasion as he was coming out of the urinal he found himself face to face with Lord Wharfedale who was engrossed in undoing his flies and was obviously not intending to acknowledge him.

'Er,' said Bognor.

His Lordship looked up with more than a hint of irritation.

'Er,' repeated Bognor. 'Could I have a word with you?'

Lord Wharfedale was clearly in a hurry. 'Tomorrow,' he rasped. 'Ten-thirty sharp,' and disappeared at the double in the direction of the drainpipe. Bognor wondered if he was on the right track. It could be unfortunate if he wasn't.

By the time the inevitable had happened and the Terrapins had reached the final, the floodlights had been switched on. The boisterous atmosphere had achieved remarkable proportions considering the cold. Several people had started to be sick, notably a party of Scotsmen in kilts who had taken up a position behind one set of goalposts where they were consuming bottles of neat whisky. They were in particularly good spirits since their team, playing prosaically under the title of 'A Scottish Seven', were the other finalists. Bognor and Molly Mortimer found a seat on the end of a bench near the half-way line and settled down to watch. Bognor hoped fervently that the Terrapins were beaten. He had no wish to have Willy Wimbledon flaunting his false modesty around the office.

Molly seemed to sense his mood because she said, 'I'm not absolutely certain I want Willy to do well. And I do wish those little girls would stop.' She was referring to the Viscount's fan club who were chanting nearby in almost as frenzied a state as the Scots behind the goalposts.

Alas, Bognor had to concede that Wimbledon was a natural ball player. From the first moment of the game he played quite beautifully. He swayed and he swerved, he executed deft little drop kicks and dexterous chips, sold dummies in all directions and shimmied about in a dazzling display. By half time the Terrapins led by twelve points and the little girls were becoming hysterical. One of the Scots had thrown a bottle on the pitch and a policeman had escorted him away amid jovial jeers. At the beginning of the second half a Scottish player hoisted an immense kick in the direction of Wimbledon who caught it and ran thirty yards to score under the posts. One of the little girls ran onto the pitch and pulled at his jersey. Two policemen chased her off. The crowd booed and cheered. A man with a hunting horn blew an erratic call and was answered by a dolorous skirl of bagpipes from the drunken Scots.

Willy was going to take the conversion kick. It was an easy one—the easiest so far and he had succeeded with both his previous attempts. He placed the ball on its end in front of the posts and walked back a few paces with studied nonchalance, brushed a golden lock from his eyes and turned to stand in a moment's concentration before running up to kick. Then an extraordinary thing happened.

The crowd, in the best traditions of British middle-class sportsmanship, had grown silent in order to let him concentrate. Even the supporters of the Scottish Seven were muted for the kick. Anyone ignorant or boorish enough to talk was quickly quietened by an admonitory 'Shhh'. But, just as the Viscount stood on tiptoe, preparatory to running three paces and kicking, there was a shout from someone standing on the touchline about ten yards to Bognor's left. Amid the hush the single word was unmistakable. 'Fairy!' The effect on Wimbledon was remarkable. He faltered and stopped and turned back again. He looked suddenly ashen. Once more he attempted a run up and again the voice called out 'Fairy!' Again he faltered but this time he managed to continue. The kick was hopelessly sliced and went miles wide, the two touch judges waved their flags at knee level to indicate failure and the crowd erupted into babble.

'Who the hell was it?' asked Bognor, staring down the line to where the shout had come from. A scuffle had broken out and even as they watched a policeman intervened to restore order. 'It sounded like . . .'

'It was,' said Molly, also staring. 'It was Granny Gringe.'

The policeman was leading Mr Gringe away. It didn't look as if he was under arrest. In fact it was more likely that the policeman was protecting Gringe from the fury of the crowd, but it wasn't the question of arrest which riveted Bognor's attention. It was the expression on Gringe's face, an expression of utter fury and hatred. He looked almost zombie-like. His eyes stared ferociously, his mouth twitched and his rogue eyebrow was once more on the blink. Bognor quite expected him to start frothing at any moment.

'Good God,' said Bognor involuntarily, 'what on earth's got into him?'

For once even Molly seemed to have lost her cool. 'Amazing,' she said. 'Amazing. I've never seen him like that. I've never seen anyone like that. He looks bonkers.' He and the policeman passed a few feet in front of them but Gringe didn't notice them. Bognor had the firm impression that if he had looked at them, even from a range of three feet, he wouldn't have seen them. He seemed to be in a trance.

'Anyway,' said Molly, 'what did he mean, "Fairy"?'

'Poof, queer, faggot, homosexual, I imagine,' said Bognor, 'unless he was referring to his style of play.'

'That's ridiculous,' she said. 'He's none of those things. I've proved it.'

'He might be,' said Bognor, 'if it suited him.'

'I think we'd better tell Bertie,' she said. 'He'll have to take over. Granny's never going to hold the column together now.'

'No wait,' said Bognor, 'I have a feeling this is about to get interesting.'

Play had restarted and was progressing in an inconclusive fashion with no particular advantage to either side. Then the Terrapin scrum-half passed the ball to Wimbledon. It was a perfect pass, straight into Wimbledon's hands. Even Bognor would have caught it eas-

ily and under normal circumstances Wimbledon would
have pocketed it and set off upfield on an elusive jink-
ing run. This time he dropped it. The ball went straight
into his waiting hands and fell out again. As he stood
apparently mesmerized two Scots charged up, hacked
the ball on and within seconds were over the line for a
score. Sixteen—four. The Scots kicker converted. Sixteen—six. The crowd sensed a Scottish comeback and
began to roar. The bagpipes sounded a more defiant
note. Almost immediately after the resumption there
was a repetition of the incident in the Cornish match.
The largest Scotsman started lumbering straight
towards Wimbledon. This time, however, the cowardice
was more obvious. Willy simply avoided him. He made
no attempt whatever to stop the man who trundled on
for another score. Again the conversion. Sixteen—
twelve in favour of the Terrapins.

The teeny bopper girls were silenced now and the
drunken Scots behind the goalposts had set up some
dreadful Celtic chant.

'Very interesting,' said Bognor. 'Very interesting
indeed.'

'Don't be so bloody smug,' said Molly. 'What's the
matter with him?'

'He obviously doesn't like being called a fairy.' He
looked at his watch. 'Still two or three minutes,' he
said. 'I reckon there's still time for him to lose it for
them.'

The Terrapins clearly realized that something had
happened to their star. In the next move he was conspicuously avoided and the ball was fed straight to the
sprinter Bagley, who was tackled only yards short of
the line. The seconds ticked away and it seemed that
the Terrapins must hang on, however precariously, to
their slim lead. The Scotsmen, however, sensed the
new Terrapin weakness. The referee was looking at his
watch, whistle poised ready to blow for the end of the
game when the Scottish scrum-half kicked the ball as
high as he could and straight towards where Willy
Wimbledon stood in splendid isolation, yards from any

protecting team-mate. The crowd hushed as the ball hung in the air and then began to drop slowly towards the lonely Viscount. The only sound was the thunder of seven pairs of Scottish boots pounding towards him. The ball, Willy and the Scots all met at the same instant. It was hardly Willy's fault this time though a tougher braver man might have clung on desperately. Instead he made a frantic grab at it, seemed for a moment to have caught it and was then brushed aside as the ball ran loose and was successfully seized by a triumphant Scot. The rest was a formality. The latest score made it level pegging at sixteen all but the conversion was as easy as the one with which Willy had failed. The crowd held its breath as the Scottish kicker ran up and clipped the ball neatly and precisely between the uprights. Eighteen—sixteen to the Scots.

The second the ball arc-ed through the posts, the touch judges waved their flags aloft signalling triumph, the referee blew a prolonged final blast on the whistle and the onlookers erupted into cheers, boos and indeterminate rhubarb noises. Some of the little girls, who minutes earlier had been so ecstatically euphoric, were now sobbing with distress and lost illusions, while two of the drunken Scots, roared on by their fellows, were attempting to climb the goal-posts.

Bognor allowed himself the luxury of a thin smile.

'I don't somehow think,' he said, smugly, 'that that will be remembered as Viscount Wimbledon's finest hour,' he said.

'Pig,' said Molly. 'He was upset.'

'I know,' said Bognor, 'and all because Eric Gringe called him a Fairy. Tut tut. Poor little fellow.'

Molly gave him a beady look. 'If you go on gloating,' she said, 'I shan't make anything up to you. Come on. Let's find Bertie.'

They tracked Bertie down by the Wharfedale dormobile/grandstand where he was putting on his dutiful heir apparent act, drinking Dimple Haig whisky and being nice to the editors. The two teams of finalists were there too, drinking non-vintage champagne, some of it from the absurd Wharfedale trophy, which had just been presented. It had been a muted presentation because Lord Wharfedale thought anything else would be too like the Cup Final of which he disapproved. He considered it common. The only player conspicuously absent was Viscount Wimbledon.

'Collar-bone,' said the Terrapin captain tersely, on being questioned, 'someone kicked it in that last maul.'

'Ah,' said Bognor. He privately thought it unlikely to be worse than a bruise. Probably inflicted by one of his own side too. He had decided that Willy was too wet to have murdered anyone. Unless . . . It didn't require much courage to push someone on a crowded platform, or smash a fist into the face of a very drunken Board of Trade investigator. The paper knife stabbing was different. And why had his game gone so totally to pieces when Gringe shouted Fairy?

'Bad luck,' said Bognor to the Terrapin captain. 'Not winning. I thought you had it sewn up.'

'So we did.' The Terrapin grimaced. He had blood on his left knee cap. 'Until Willy went to bits. I don't understand it. The second that fellow shouted out "Fairy" he cracked up.'

Bognor shrugged. He noticed that Molly was in deep and earnest talk with Bertie Harris who was wearing an expression of ritual concern, rather like a doctor trying out a new bedside manner.

After a few minutes of sage nodding and shaking Bertie knocked back his Scotch with a flourish, waved at Bognor to follow and marched off with Molly in the direction of the press tent.

The next hour and half was devoted to constructing a column. Gringe was nowhere to be seen, nor Wimbledon, and Milborn Port was quietly gibbering. However Gringe's insistence on as much copy as possible by lunch, had paid dividends. Bognor himself had already written notes on the Earl of Surrey, the Plynlimmon Goat, Freddie ffrench-Patrick, and the Seven Sisters' Stompers. These and other similar offerings about rugger players with withered legs, rugger players who had won VCs, rugger players who had gone off with other rugger players' wives, rugger players who had become Bishops of the Church of England and an improbable anecdote from Milborn Port about the popularity of rugger at the Vatican had all been telephoned to the *Globe* during the afternoon by the temporary secretary. There Horace Peckwater had perused them and amended them and checked them and placed them in order and constructed suitable headlines for each one.

Nevertheless there was more to do, and the three members of the Pepys staff who remained sober and intact addressed themselves to the difficult task of writing more items about the day's entertainment. It was slow work. However, well before the deadline time of approximately six o'clock Bertie expressed reasonable satisfaction. Just as they were finishing and preparing to retire to the next door tent for a final drink before going home Viscount Wimbledon appeared. He looked wan and sheepish and held his heavily bandaged arm in a sling made from the silk scarf he had earlier worn round his neck.

A chorus of 'Oh, I say, bad luck, old boy,' 'Hard cheese', and similarly hypocritical condolences greeted his arrival. Secretly everyone was as amused as Bognor by his discomfiture but no one quite had the gall to show it.

'Where's Gringe?' he asked. No one knew and there was a general embarrassed shuffling. No answer. Finally he looked at Bognor and said with a show of bravado, 'I owe you a drink, if you'd still like it?'

'Fine,' he said.

The beer tent was now distinctly seedy. The few drinkers left were in poor shape and the staff, grown surly after the day's work, showed signs of restiveness. Had the Pepys people not arrived when they did the tent would have been struck and the remaining clients tidied away with the rubbish. Conversation was strained. Bognor was ill at ease himself and also keen to see Gringe. He wondered what it was that the wretched man had wanted to tell him and also what explanation he would offer for his effective cry of 'Fairy'.

'I did enjoy some of your earlier stuff,' he said tentatively to Wimbledon. 'Pity about the final. I almost got the impression that . . .'

'I'd rather not talk about it if you don't mind,' said the Viscount. He was still obviously upset but, Bognor reckoned, more by the 'Fairy' remark than the loss of face or final.

'Did you manage to get a good column together?'

'All right. I had a chat with your father.'

'Yes.'

The silences became longer until they almost obliterated speech. In the middle of a particularly long one there was the scrunch of feet on empty beer cans and a bemacintoshed figure appeared in the door of the tent. Mr Gringe steadied himself briefly with one hand on a conveniently placed guy rope.

'Ah,' he said. His face was in the shadow but it was clear from the way he was standing that he was very unsure of himself.

'My round,' said Bognor with a brightness he didn't feel. 'What's yours?'

'I'd like a brandy if I may, please.'

Bognor ordered the brandy and beers for everyone else. The brandy was presumably medicinal but it was also twice as expensive as beer and its ordering irritated Bognor, and, he guessed, everyone else. The hostility was almost tangible. Most of it was directed at Gringe but he sensed much more. Some was aimed at himself too, but almost everyone now seemed to have at least one acknowledged enemy among his colleagues. Almost facetiously he wondered when the next murder would be done.

It almost happened immediately, and might have done if the two protagonists weren't so emotionally and physically unwell. Wimbledon, coping clumsily with a cigarette, a pint tankard and his sling, sidled across to Granny Gringe and said with all the menace of

Humphrey Bogart: 'Would you mind stepping outside a minute. I have something I want to say.' There was no mistaking the threat in his tones and since, despite the stage whisper, everyone else was listening and watching, it was clear to all of them.

Gringe drank brandy, his hand shaking as he raised the glass so that a tiny trickle missed his mouth and ran down his chin and on to the collar of his raincoat.

'I'm not going outside with you,' he said. The words were innocuous enough but he managed to imply that if he had gone outside he would have been instantly subjected to a sexual assault. Wimbledon didn't miss the innuendo.

'In that case I'll have to say it here, where everyone can hear.'

'Go ahead.' It was too dark to see Gringe's eyebrows but Bognor would not have been surprised to discover that they were both performing acrobatics.

'I say, you two.' It was Bertie Harris falling into the role of elder statesman and heir to the Empire again. 'Don't you think all this ought to wait till tomorrow? We have had a very long day and it's been pretty bloody difficult. Now why don't you just pack it in and talk about it in the morning when we've had a chance to sleep on it?'

'Bugger that,' said Wimbledon, his voice rising. His beer was spilling and he put it down on a table so that he could use his hand for the cigarette. It glowed in the shadows as he jabbed it towards Gringe's nose. Then he seemed to subside again.

'It doesn't matter,' he said, 'I'll just say one thing and that is that I'm resigning. I'm not working under you, you sneaky little voyeur. You can have it in writing tomorrow. Goodnight.'

And he was gone. The cigarette end lay where he'd thrown it in a pile of litter, still glowing for a few moments while everyone gazed blankly and speechlessly at the darkened entrance out of which he had vanished.

'He'll be all right in the morning,' said Bertie with a humourless laugh. 'Nothing like a good night's sleep to restore some perspective. I think it really is time we went.'

It was, too. The staff had been banging empty crates about for five minutes and now stood staring at them with undisguised resentment. They left, chorusing goodnights to each other as they did and making their way independently towards the car park.

Bognor caught Granny Gringe about fifty yards out of the tent.

'You wanted to talk to me,' he said.

'Yes,' said Gringe, 'but I think I've changed my mind.'

'It's too late,' said Bognor. 'You're involved now. You know something and I want to be in on the secret. Do you have a car?'

'I came by train to Barnes.'

'Where are you going now?'

'Bromley.'

'From Blackfriars?'

'Yes.'

'I'll give you a lift. We can talk in the car.'

'I don't want to talk. I've changed my mind.' His voice was beginning to go out of control again.

'You don't have any option. This is a murder enquiry. And you know something. You can't withhold evidence.'

'That's ridiculous.'

'It's true.'

They had arrived at the pavilion now. The lights were on inside and through the windows they could see the merry throng of rugger hearties gathered round the bar elbows bent as they drank their pints. A vigorous chorus of 'Eskimo Nell' came wafting out on the chill night air.

'It'll take you hours to get home on public transport,' said Bognor, 'and it's a bloody night.'

He took a minute to make up his mind, then he said, sadly and softly, 'All right. It'll have to come out in the end.'

They turned and walked away from the raucous

singing to the car park. Neither said anything until Bognor had negotiated the busy crossroads near the Red Rover pub and was heading east towards Putney.

'Well,' he said eventually, settling into fourth gear behind an articulated lorry from Belgium, 'I've seldom seen a more effective piece of heckling. Tell me more.'

For a minute he didn't think Gringe was going to respond, and they were beyond Putney Swimming Pool before he spoke. Then without further prompting he was in full spate. It was irrelevant to murder, at least irrelevant to the mechanics of murder although it provided a sort of motive. 'You wouldn't understand,' he began, and Bognor knew then that he would be forced to understand willy-nilly. For ten minutes Gringe kept up a ceaseless diatribe. He catalogued his own parentage, childhood, adolescence: The sacrifices to send him to grammar school, to red brick university; the hours of extra study, the newspaper round, the vacation jobs, labouring; his army service, fighting for a commission in the Pay Corps; then journalism; the court reporting on the local paper; the promotion to a big regional paper in Newcastle; the big break which sent him across country to join the *Globe*'s Manchester staff as a news reporter, the years of drudgery and then another break when he scooped the rest of the country's papers with his exclusive revelations of embezzlement and perjury in one of the country's largest trade unions; the implausible reward of a job in London on the Samuel Pepys column and the humiliating discovery there of the privileged. He had sweated blood and ink to get there and when he arrived what did he find? He found men who had been born to it, men who had inherited it, men who were doing it because they could think of nothing else to do with their rotten worthless lives, men with titles, men who squandered and frittered such meagre talents as they possessed on women and horses and above all alcohol, reducing themselves to privileged parasites, a perpetual affront to the honest, the poor, the industrious, to people like himself who by their own toil and guts and talent had pulled themselves up and made something of themselves.

They were at Battersea Dogs' Home before he paused for breath. Bognor seized the opportunity mercilessly.

'But Viscount Wimbledon,' he said. 'You called him a fairy.'

It was an advantage, he realized, that he had Gringe to himself in the car and that it was dark. He couldn't see his face except occasionally when they paused near a brighter than usual street lamp and this gave Gringe confidence and anonymity. He was almost talking to himself.

'Worthless, worthless Willy,' he said, sounding more than a little hysterical and giving a shrill demented laugh. 'You've seen him, with his little kiss curl and his bloody blues and his title and his privilege. But I found out. I found out.'

'How?'

Gringe stopped short, suddenly embarrassed again. He asked for a cigarette though Bognor had never seen him smoke before, and when Bognor had lit it for him, sucked inexpertly on it, coughing and not inhaling. When he spoke again it was with his usual diffidence but it quickly evaporated.

'It was one evening a few months ago. St John said he was ill. I thought he was hung over. He said in the morning that he wouldn't be coming to work but he'd like to see the column in the evening if I'd care to drop it in on my way home. He knew perfectly well that his flat wasn't on my way home. It was in the other direction. But he didn't care about me. He thought I was common, insignificant, nothing. He'd made something of himself all right. He'd sold out. All that nonsense about the cane and the cloak and the plummy voice and the smart friends. He was a toad, a common toad.'

He coughed and rolled down the window, then threw the half finished cigarette out and rolled it up again.

'But Wimbledon,' prompted Bognor. 'You said he was a fairy?'

'I took the copy round,' he said. 'All of it. All eleven stories. And he'd forgotten I was coming. I could tell by the time it took him to answer. I rang twice and then when he came he looked upset and anxious and surprised. He looked as if he'd been caught red-handed. "Come in, dear boy," he said, like he always did, only he didn't mean it, you could tell by his eyes. But I went in, just to spite him, even though he didn't want it. He was wearing a dressing gown. Silk with golden dragons on it and nothing underneath. I could tell something was wrong, so I went in.'

Bognor narrowly missed a parked car. He was enjoying the story.

'And . . .' he said.

'Nothing for a minute or two. He gave me a glass of sherry. Dry sherry, so dry it was almost like vinegar. He knew I liked it sweet but it was his way of upstaging me, making me feel small and stupid. And he read the column but I could tell he was nervous by the way he kept fidgeting, and then *he* came in.'

'Who?' Bognor knew perfectly well, but he wanted to savour it.

'Little Lord Fauntleroy, Worthless Willy Wimbledon.'

'And that was the first time you saw him, before he got the job on the column.'

'That's why he got the job on the column, isn't it? For services rendered.'

'And you never told anyone?'

They were at Lambeth now, just passing the Archbishop's palace, with the Houses of Parliament silhouetted across the river on their left. He felt Gringe hesitate.

'No,' he said finally. 'Well, that is I told one person, only that was different. It's what I wanted to talk to you about earlier.'

'Ah.' It was what Bognor had been half expecting. Another bit of jigsaw was fitting into place, though there were still a lot of pieces to go. He tried to make it easier.

'You told Anthea Morrison?'

'How did you know?'

'I guessed. You forget I'm a professional.' Bognor didn't feel like it, and to be honest he had only really guessed a few minutes earlier. It was the signal for another outpouring of frustration and disillusion and hatred and pent-up emotion. Through the torrent of words Bognor managed to single out the salient facts. Gringe disliked his wife who was prissy and pushy, and wanted him to be, God knows what, Editor, King, Prime Minister. Or more precisely *she* wanted to be Queen. And as Bognor had observed, and as Gringe knew all too clearly, Eric Gringe was one of life's losers. In the office which he so clearly loathed there was only one person who was similarly patronized and ignored and who suffered the ignominy of being thought lower class. That was Anthea Morrison. Their affair had blossomed slowly, if only because Gringe was a man of chronically nervous disposition and little initiative. Anthea was a Catholic and that hardly helped. Nevertheless they had begun to see each other. At first it was totally harmless. When the others were off drinking at El Vino or the American Bar at the Savoy or Jules in Jermyn Street, then Eric and Anthea would snatch a quick coffee in one of the small shops off Ludgate Circus. The relationship remained platonic though inevitably Derby, who missed nothing, realized that something was going on and used Gringe's pathological nervousness and fear of his wife to indulge his tiresome habit of blackmail. There was little money involved but it seemed that Derby was like the little boy who enjoys pulling wings off insects. He couldn't resist tormenting the guilty.

However the relationship was manageable until Gringe received an invitation to a gastronomic weekend at the Grand in Brighton. Originally he and Mrs Gringe were to go but she developed some gastric infection on the Friday and cried off. Gringe still had to go and asked Anthea Morrison. It was not intended to be a suggestive invitation. Gringe did not think of himself as sexually desirable, nor Anthea as sexually attainable, but the inevitable happened. She accepted and after a nine course banquet and a lot to drink the two of them ended up in the double bed originally intended for Mr and Mrs Gringe. Neither had taken any precautions. They had been too drunk and too surprised and anyway Anthea was a Catholic. Next day they were both full of half-hearted recriminations but it was too late. Miss Morrison was pregnant. Later when she discovered, she refused to have the abortion for which Gringe pleaded. She had resolved to have the child and let it be adopted.

'So you see,' said Mr Gringe, as they sat in the car, now parked by the side of Blackfriars station. 'I am your man.'

'I'm sorry, what?' said Bognor, who had been listening, enthralled.

Gringe asked for another cigarette which he handled as clumsily and with as little enjoyment as the first.

'When I found out about Viscount Wimbledon and St John,' he said, morosely, 'I thought I'd get my own back. I went to him and I said that if he told anyone about me and Anthea I'd tell everyone about him and Willy.'

'And?'

'And,' Gringe's voice here became positively tremulous, 'he laughed.'

'So.'

'I went on paying the money.'

'And you think you'll be accused of murdering St John Derby because he was blackmailing you?'

Mr Gringe said nothing coherent but a stifled sob emerged from his direction and Bognor saw that he was nodding.

'If you want to know,' said Bognor, 'the late St John Derby was blackmailing half London. There's hardly a man alive without a good reason for having knifed him.'

'But there's Anthea,' wailed Gringe. 'They'll say I killed her because she was going to have my child and then I'd have been ruined.' He broke off and began to sob uncontrollably, coughing at the same time on the unfamiliar tobacco smoke. When, eventually, he stopped, Bognor asked him a question.

'Why did you wear that frightful macintosh to the Sevens today?'

Gringe looked at him as if he was insane. 'It was cold and I thought it might rain or snow.'

'Don't you have a proper overcoat?'

'No.'

'And you didn't think of wearing a hat?'

'I don't have a hat.'

Bognor leant across and opened his door for him. 'Come on,' he said, 'I'll walk to the train with you. Otherwise you'll miss it and your wife will give you hell.'

'Aren't you going to . . . don't you want to ask . . . I mean,' Mr Gringe seemed strangely disappointed. Almost as if he had been hoping for handcuffs and a prison cell.

'I'm sorry,' said Bognor, 'I don't think you killed anybody. Somehow you're going to have to carry on living. I'm sorry.'

He saw him onto his train but neither of them said any more, except for a mumbled goodnight. The carriage was almost empty and Mr Gringe sat on a corner seat near the window, fidgeting with another cigarette Bognor had given him. Bognor watched as the train drew out, slowly taking away the forlorn, crumpled figure in his distinctive dirty mackintosh.

'Poor little sod,' said Bognor under his breath.

8

At home he found Monica in more forgiving mood. She poured him a drink and ran a bath, then listened to the day's events.

'Sounds like more motives,' she said, when he'd finished. 'Everyone has one now. If I were you I'd leave
it to the police.'

Bognor frowned. 'No,' he said slowly. 'I think I
rather agree with Bertie Harris and his father. If left to
their own devices the police are going to pick the
wrong man. If I know Gringe he'll have cracked up
even more overnight. I wouldn't put it past him to
confess to Sanders in the morning. If he does then the
only piece of hard evidence against him is some cir-
cumstantial stuff about a man in an overcoat and hat
seen pushing away from the crowd at Blackfriars underground station. And Gringe's only defence is that he
always wears a mac. No one's going to accept that.'

'But you do,' said Monica.

'It's not that,' he said. 'I just believe someone else is
guilty. And I think I know who.'

Before he went to bed Bognor put a phone call
through to his old Oxford acquaintance, Spencer
Nugent, political editor of the *Daily News*.

'It's a tall order,' said Spencer when he'd explained
what he wanted, 'but I'll see what I can do. I'll ring
you tomorrow morning at the *Globe*.'

In bed Bognor said, quite seriously, 'If this doesn't
work then I think Parkinson will, as they say, "have
my guts for garters".'

He slept badly. The images which disturbed his slum-
bers were manifold. The staff of the Samuel Pepys
column paraded before him with bloodied paper
knives, each one of them in turn. He saw St John
Derby on a step ladder hiding pieces of evidence in the
cricketers' almanacks, and turning to address him with
a triumphant leer: 'Eric Gringe has got the secretary
pregnant, Viscount Wimbledon has been to bed with
me, "Sir" Milborn Port sells dirty stories to the Russians, Bertie Harris is selling his inheritance for a mess
of pottage, and dear Molly here is my willing accom-
plice.' Then he declaimed:

In the city set upon slime and loam
They cry in their parliament 'Who goes home?'
And there comes no answer in arch or dome
For none in the city of graves goes home.

And with a final ghastly cackle he fell off the ladder clutching a paper knife to his stomach, and Bognor woke.

Before his interview with Lord Wharfedale he looked in briefly at the Samuel Pepys office where, to his surprise, he found everyone present and correct, albeit self-consciously silent.

'Might I have a word, Willy,' he asked the youth whose only sign of yesterday's adventures was the silk sling which supported his injured arm. Wimbledon followed him into the corridor.

'Eric Gringe told me,' said Bognor brusquely. 'I assume you thought that by seducing St John you'd make sure of a job and a future.'

'It wasn't like that,' he said, surlily. 'You won't tell Molly, will you?' He showed no sign of shame. Bognor was offended.

'If you want to reach the Editor's chair on your back that's your business,' he said loftily, 'but I do need to know for certain that it was you who slugged me outside Molly's flat. And if you don't tell me the truth I'll make sure the whole of Fleet Street knows you got your job by sleeping with St John. Then you really will have to resign.'

To his gratification the Viscount winced. 'I told you,' he said, 'I thought you and Molly . . .' his voice trailed off.

'I believe you,' said Bognor, 'but if you're lying, then I'll do exactly what I said.'

Upstairs at half past ten he went through the complex ritual of gaining admittance to Lord Wharfedale and was pleased to see the same nubile blonde secretary wearing the same white trouser suit. His Lordship was smoking a Havana.

'You may have four minutes thirty-five seconds, Bognor,' he said, gazing out of the window across Fleet Street towards Holborn. 'I'm a busy man.'

'I only have two questions,' he said. 'They won't take long. First of all, did you at any stage try to get rid of St John Derby?'

Lord Wharfedale turned to stare at Bognor, which he did with a look clearly designed to turn lesser men to stone or into pillars of salt. Bognor found it unimpressive. He looked like an angry overweight monkey. Eventually, sensing that his menacing stare was not having the desired effect he said, 'St John Derby was a very remarkable man. I've said so before. I said it in the newspaper. I may say it again at his memorial service. God rest his soul.'

'But did you want to sack him?'

'Maybe I did.' He smiled an evil little smile and waved his cigar in the air. 'Comes a time, Mr Bognor, as you will find to your cost one day, when a man is but a shadow of his former self. "The Lord giveth and the Lord taketh away"; and to be absolutely frank with you, Mr Bognor, in my opinion St John Derby had reaped his talents. I would have preferred to see him enjoying a peaceful retirement.'

'But the Union stopped you.'

'Hell and damnation, no. The Union is a powerful creature. You flout it at your peril. But even the Union doesn't interfere with my hiring and my firing.'

'Then why didn't you fire St John Derby?'

'You really want to know?'

'Yes.'

'Are you going to tell me why?'

'Later today I may.'

'That's very good of you.' Lord Wharfedale's sarcasm was considerable. He continued: 'If you really want to know, St John Derby stayed on this paper because of the kindness and affection of my son, Bertie, who appreciated his virtues perhaps more than I did.'

Bognor said nothing, then saw that he was expected to speak.

'And you accepted your son's assessment. You let him keep Mr Derby on when you yourself wanted him out?'

Lord Wharfedale looked ruminative.

'Odd thing, Mr Bognor,' he said after a moment. 'For years I listened to Bertie but finally I decided that St John Derby would have to go, no matter what Bertie thought. I told Bertie I would finally give him the golden handshake on Thursday morning. Now there's an odd thing.'

'See you later,' said Bognor flippantly, rising to go. He felt oddly optimistic.

Downstairs once more he found that there was no one left in the Pepys office except for the temporary secretary. He assumed they were all out drinking.

'Two messages for you, Mr Bognor,' she said, smiling a spotty smile and pulling her skirts down round her fleshy thighs. 'Mr Nugent says your interview is arranged for twelve noon and Mr Sanders has just telephoned to say, could he see you in the front hall. He said it's urgent.'

In the front hall Sanders was examining the bust of Lord Wharfedale with an expression of truculence. His earlier friendliness seemed to have evaporated after the débâcle at St John Derby's old flat.

'You can go back to your work now,' he said brusquely, 'and stop playing at detectives. We've got our man.'

'Oh?'

'Gringe. He's just been in my office making a confession and I've sent him down to the station to get it all done according to the book, have him charged and get everything typed out and witnessed.' He paused and smiled. 'Well,' he continued, holding out his hand, 'I wish I could say what a help you've been but I'm afraid your intervention wasn't exactly a success. Never mind. In future perhaps everyone will remember to leave matters of life and death to the professionals. Luckily you didn't do any real damage. But you could have done.'

Bognor ignored the outstretched hand.

'You're wrong,' he said. 'He didn't do it.'

'Look,' Sanders was giving the impression of the man whose patience, sorely tried, is about to be exhausted. 'We've got it all. He was having an affair with the secretary. Derby found out and was blackmailing him so he arranged a late night meeting to thrash the thing out, and, when there was a row stabbed him with the paper knife which was lying on the desk. Then he pushed the secretary under the train because she wouldn't have an abortion, also because she knew about the murder.'

'How?'

'He told her.'

Bognor couldn't conceal his impatience.

'I thought you were tolerably intelligent,' he snapped. 'He couldn't possibly have done it.'

'And why not?' Sanders's voice was rising too.

'Because he owns a grubby mackintosh and no overcoat and because somebody else did it.'

'You stick to *Wisden Cricketers' Almanacks*,' shouted the policeman so that everyone in the front hall heard and glanced up. He flounced across to the swing doors and marched out with an air of wronged authority.

'Ass,' said Bognor.

Back in the Pepys office, he wondered how he was going to handle his interview at noon. It was the most crucial of the case and if it misfired it would be disastrous.

As he was sitting contemplating, Bertie, Willy, Milly and Molly came in together. They had evidently heard. Indeed as soon as Bognor's back was turned Granny Gringe had apparently treated them to a dummy run confession. All of them seemed deeply impressed, with the exception of Molly Mortimer who was strangely quiet. After the others had had their say, each one being wise after the event with much protestations about always knowing 'there was something funny about Granny', she said nonchalantly:

'Simon darling, would you fancy lunch at the Montegufoni?'

'That would be nice but . . .'

'I said I'd make it up to you.'

He smiled. 'I'd imagined it would be more interesting than lunch.'

She didn't smile back. 'I wanted to talk to you about cricket,' she said.

He arrived at the front hall of the *Daily News* at five to twelve. It didn't do to keep Managing Editors and heirs apparent waiting. It was a less grandiose building than that of the *Globe*, situated in a side street which ran from Fleet Street down to the Thames Embankment. There was none of the gilded flamboyance he associated with the Wharfedale group. Instead there was a lot of plate glass functionalism, electric doors which slid rather than manual ones which swung, and an abundance of garish strip lighting. The only point of similarity was the gnarled uniformed figure at the reception desk who seemed identical to the one at the *Globe*.

He addressed himself to this individual and was told to go to the fifth floor where Mr Gravelle's secretary would meet him. The lift was modern and it worked. Gravelle's secretary was crisp, clean, functional and worked as efficiently as the lift. She showed him straight into Gravelle's office which was completely free of ostentation.

Gravelle showed no sign of recognition from lunch at Pring's. Bognor produced his identity card, which he studied cursorily.

'I've no doubt that you are who you say you are,' he said, smoothing back neat, jet black hair, 'but I'm at a loss as to what you could possibly want to see me about.'

Bognor took a very deep breath.

'It's about a possible merger between this group and the Wharfedale Organization.'

'Yes.' Elliston Gravelle picked up a ruler and bent it to just short of snapping point.

'I wanted to know whether this was going to take place?'

'Surely that's a matter for the Monopolies Commission rather than the Board of Trade?'

'In a sense, yes, but I do have an interest in the matter.'

'Would you mind telling me what that interest might be?'

'I must ask you to treat what I'm going to say as a matter of the utmost confidence.' Bognor hated it when he started to assume the outward pomposities of the professional civil servant.

'Naturally.'

Another deep breath. Bognor was aware that he was on exceedingly dangerous ground. One false move and Elliston Gravelle would be on the phone to Parkinson or, worse still, the Minister. And that would be the end.

'I have information that an agreement between you and the Honourable Bertie Harris has already been signed to the effect that a merger will take place in the event of your inheriting your fathers' respective organizations.'

'Oh.'

'And I'd like that information confirmed.'

'I'm afraid,' Mr Gravelle did not look in the least afraid, 'that that is not the sort of information I am prepared to discuss with you.'

'Even if it were an integral part of a murder enquiry?'

Mr Gravelle looked as if he were about to say 'Pish, Tush', but changed his mind and instead said, 'Would you kindly elaborate?'

Bognor began to get very cold feet indeed.

'I have reason to suspect,' he said very deliberately, 'that a certain person, now deceased, was aware of such an agreement between you and Mr Harris and was using it for the purposes of blackmail.'

'And how might that have been achieved?'

'If either your father or Lord Wharfedale were to discover that their heir was going to sell out to a rival they would be quite likely to disinherit that heir.'

'It's conceivable.'

'So I want to know whether such an agreement is in existence.'

Elliston Gravelle continued to play with the ruler. Eventually he said: 'I'm sorry, Mr . . . er Bognor, but I am unable to help you.'

'But this *is* a murder enquiry.'

'If, Mr Bognor, it is a murder enquiry, I will be happy to answer any questions from the proper authority which in this case is the police. However I am not able to discuss commerical matters relating to the future of this company with officials from the Board of Trade. I'm sorry.'

'I'm sorry too.'

'Good-bye, Mr Bognor, thank you for coming.'

'But . . .'

'*Good-bye*, Mr Bognor.'

He was angry now. Angry principally because he was increasingly certain that he was right, and increasingly afraid that he was going to be foiled. Perhaps Gringe, with all his talk of privilege, had been right. Perhaps the strong would survive while poor old Eric, the honest toiler of modest origins, would go to the wall. He knew now why he thought Bertie was the murderer. Not because of the feeble lie about sacking Derby although that was crucial, but because he could feel the Establishment closing ranks already. Elliston Gravelle had signed that agreement. He was sure of it, but Gravelle was going to protect his old mucker from Oxford. And the police with the easy option of choosing Gringe would hardly try to pin a murder on such a celebrated and privileged Establishment figure as Bertie.

He walked back to the *Globe* in a trance. It was so plain. Bertie had told him that his father wanted to sack Derby because he thought he would find out any-way, but had he let on that he had been defending the indefensible he would have laid himself open to suspicion. So he pretended that the Union had objected to his sacking. It was a plausible enough theory, and with the welter of other suspects he could reasonably reckon to get away with it. Dammit, thought Bognor, he nearly has got away with it.

Clearly his father had told him that he was on the point of overruling him and firing Derby. And he knew that the instant Derby was fired he would blow the gaffe on the deal that Bertie had arranged with Elliston Gravelle. Those must have been the terms of the blackmail. Derby would keep quiet about the deal so long as he remained on the paper, despite his obvious inadequacies. And it was up to Bertie to make sure he wasn't fired. Not a bad deal.

He wondered how he had discovered the agreement and found himself laughing. Old St John was obviously a better journalist than most people had thought. The trouble was his talents had been deployed on extra mural activities. And then there was poor Anthea Morrison. She must have got in the way somewhere . . .

'You're late.' It was Molly Mortimer. He had forgotten. They had a lunch date at the Montegufoni. What was it that she'd said? He'd been too preoccupied to notice. Something about cricket. Cricket? *Wisden Cricketers' Almanacks*. He gave a little gasp of hope.

The Montegufoni was a lunch club rather than a restaurant and it overlooked the Thames near Dolphin Square, more than a quarter of an hour's drive from Fleet Street. The clients were principally showbiz types, the decor gilt and velvet, the food expensive prawn cocktail and scampi. They sat in a window and looked out at the mud. Until the steaks, which were expensive, uncompromising but identifiable as beef and not instantly re-heated spun protein, they talked about nothing. Bognor wished he didn't find her so attractive.

Finally she said: 'It was me, I'm afraid.'

'What?'

'Who locked you in Derby's flat.'

'But why?'

'What else could I do?'

'Maybe, but why were you there?'

'To remove the evidence. I thought the police might have it but they'd obviously been too stupid so I thought I'd do everyone a favour.'

He was suspicious and showed it. On the other hand he was sufficiently infatuated to phrase the question kindly. 'When you say "do everyone a favour", you don't mean "do yourself a favour"?'

She chewed a piece of gristle. 'You don't mean . . . Oh Simon. For Christ's sake I'd no idea you had such a suspicious mind. I'm a nice lady. I don't do that sort of thing.'

'But how did you know where to look?'

'I told you I rumbled Derby once and I had an affair with him, in the old days before he went over to sleeping with poor little rich boys.' She gave an elegant snort of disgust. 'I just knew where to look.'

'And . . .'

She chewed more steak. 'Bloody tough, this,' she said. 'Anyway, I've burnt most of it. Not without reading it I hasten to add. Bloody marvellous stuff it was too. No wonder he was so stinking rich. There was enough there to keep the *News of the World* in stories for years. And bring down half a dozen governments. He was good at his job, I'll say that for him.'

'But not good at his other job. At the *Globe*.'

'That wasn't a job, that was a front. Anyway I said "most of it". I've kept one little document because the more I looked at it and the more I thought about it, the more I realized that it was probably what you wanted. I may be wrong, but I think not. Intuition's my strong point.'

She reached down to her handbag and pulled out a photostat of a legal document. Bognor ran his eye swiftly down it to the signatures. The two principals were The Honourable Bertie Harris and Elliston Grav-

elle, and the witness below Harris's name was Anthea
Morrison. It provided for the acquisition of the
Wharfedale Empire by the *News* Group. There were
some face-saving clauses but that was the gist of it.

Bognor gave a little whistle of triumph. 'I adore
you,' he said, 'you're magnificent.'

She shrugged. 'You agree with me then?'

'Yes.' He told her about his interviews with Wharfedale and with Elliston Gravelle. Then he looked de-
spondent. 'Doesn't prove anything on its own though,'
he said. 'The case against Granny Gringe is just as
strong; and it's not bad against Milborn or Willy when
you come to think about it.'

They drank cognac. 'You take that to Wharfedale,'
she said, 'and see what happens. If that doesn't flush
him out nothing will.'

They had more cognac. 'You're right,' he said and
went to telephone. A few minutes later he came back,
pleased. 'His secretary says five-thirty,' he said. 'Do we
have time for another cognac?'

'Why not?' she said. 'I put our names on the notice
board with the phone number. They can get hold of us
if we're needed.'

They had yet more cognac.

Outside in the blustery freezing afternoon he kissed
her. He was full of drink, lust and gratitude in equal
quantities. Then, suffering from a surfeit of gallantry
he stepped into the road to look for a taxi. He was
more drunk than she, perhaps because she was used to
it. She was lucid and level-headed and observant. He
wasn't.

As he was standing peering vacuously towards Pim-
lico he heard a powerful car accelerate towards him.
He paid no attention until suddenly he heard Molly
shout his name and then felt her strong arms reach out
and heave him back so that he fell heavily onto the
pavement. At the same time he heard a snarl of
speeding engine, felt a rush of hot air and was vaguely
aware of something pale blue whipping past only

inches in front of him. Immediately over the spot on which he had been standing an instant before.

'Christ,' he said, sitting up and gazing after the rapidly disappearing sports car. 'Bloody idiot. He might have killed me.'

'We were right,' said Molly. 'He meant to. That was a Porsche. Remember who has a pale blue Porsche?'

'Christ,' said Bognor, 'I feel sick.'

Lord Wharfedale looked more like a maniacal monkey than ever. The cigar was still there, though it appeared to have grown during the day assuming the proportions of a large brown banana, and around it his mouth was set in a petulant snarl.

'You have until Thursday morning, Mr Bognor,' he said. 'Is this interview necessary?'

'I believe so, yes sir.'

'The police have arrested Mr Gringe. Do you think it likely he perpetrated the slayings?' There were times when his Lordship sounded like an American paper of the prohibition era rather than a British one of the seventies.

'Emphatically not,' said Bognor.

'I concur,' said Lord Wharfedale.

'I have a theory,' said Bognor tentatively.

'I run a newspaper, Mr Bognor, not a think tank. We deal in facts.'

'Very well then. I'll give you the facts.' And he told him about St John Derby's nasty habit of blackmailing people, and about Bertie Harris's strange failure to mention that it was he not the Union who prevented Derby being sacked, and about the agreement to sell out the *Globe* to the *News*. At this point Lord Wharfedale's teeth clenched in such a way that Bognor feared he would bite the end off his cigar. But he said nothing.

'You told me,' Bognor concluded, 'that you would have sacked Derby on Thursday morning at which point your son would have been revealed as a secret negotiator with the opposition. So, Derby had to be removed before he could incriminate, and he was. Then

Bertie became panicky and remembered that Miss Morrison had been a witness to his signature—though I bet he never showed her exactly what it was she was signing—so he decided to make quite safe by pushing her under a train.

'And incidentally he tried to run over me in his car this afternoon. My guess is that Elliston Gravelle had tipped him off. He knew I was on the scent.'

Lord Wharfedale said nothing for a long time and it was impossible to tell what he was thinking. He evidently didn't like what he had heard because his eyebrows were knotted in a black frown and he was trying to grind his teeth round the cigar. Finally he said, 'Please wait outside until further notice.'

Normally it would have been a pleasure to wait outside with the lovely blonde secretary dimpling prettily in her white canvas, but today Bognor was apprehensive. As a parting gesture he had left the incriminating photostat on Lord Wharfedale's desk and he now realized that if family ties proved sufficiently strong the father and son could burn it and any proof would be gone for ever. And Gringe would be sentenced to life imprisonment.

He was about to despair of any development when Bertie Harris entered. He passed straight through the anteroom without looking to either side.

'Looks as if he'd seen a ghost, doesn't he?' remarked the secretary conversationally.

Presently they could hear voices. They were raised voices but the walls and the doors of Lord Wharfedale's office were so thick and impenetrable that only the occasionally angry shout could be distinguished and even then the actual word was muffled. Bognor looked at his watch. It was after six. He guessed that there might be no Samuel Pepys column tomorrow. Most of the staff had too much else on their plates.

Suddenly the shouting reached a crescendo. Bognor and the secretary looked at each other in alarm and then just as they were about to comment there was a sharp explosion.

The secretary stood up, alarmed. 'That sounded like . . .'

'A shot,' said Bognor, 'I think you're right. I have a funny feeling there may be another one in a minute. So sit tight.'

She didn't have to because as he said the words there was another bang.

'You'd better ring the police,' said Bognor coldly. 'I wouldn't go in if I were you.'

He'd had enough. He was sorry they were dead. *If* they were dead, which seemed a fair assumption. But he'd had enough. He wondered what Parkinson would say. Or Sanders. Or next morning's *Daily Globe*. 'Lord Wharfedale dead in tragic shooting accident' he expected. So much for 'The truth, the whole truth, and nothing but the truth, so help me God.'

In the front hall he met Molly Mortimer, sexy as ever in a cocoon of fur and suede.

'Well?' she asked.

He took a last look round the grandiose hall with its mad extravagant copper mural and its flamboyant motto.

'All finished,' he said. 'I'll tell you about it some other time.'

She pouted in disappointment. 'I was hoping you might come back to the flat,' she said. 'I've still got some making up to do.'

She was very alluring. Then he remembered loyal homely Monica and the safe comfortable basement at the Board of Trade. Also two lines of Chesterton.

And there comes no answer in arch or dome
For none in the city of graves goes home.

'Sorry,' he said. 'I'll see you soon,' and he kissed her sadly on the cheek. 'But I think it would be safer if I went home.'